*"It wasn't an a___
Cully said, soft___*

Her breath caught in ___
her lips move. "What happened?"

"They were shot at close range. The house looked like a tornado had gone through it. Lamps smashed, chairs overturned, drawers pulled out from dressers…a real mess."

She shuddered. "And you have no idea who it was?" Her twinge of awareness at his closeness took her by surprise. She hadn't expected to still be affected by him like this.

"Not yet." His mouth tightened in a grim line. For a long moment he kept his gaze on his hands, then slowly he raised his chin. "But I will."

Available in June 2006 from Silhouette Intrigue

Rocky Mountain Mystery
by Cassie Miles
(Colorado Crime Consultants)

Official Duty
by Doreen Roberts
(Cowboy Cops)

Hard Evidence
by Susan Peterson
(Lipstick Ltd.)

Shadows on the Lake
by Leona Karr
(Eclipse)

Official Duty

DOREEN ROBERTS

*Silhouette and Colophon are registered trademarks of
Harlequin Books S.A., used under licence.*

*First published in Great Britain 2006
Silhouette Books, Eton House, 18-24 Paradise Road,
Richmond, Surrey TW9 1SR*

© Doreen Roberts Hight 2004

ISBN 0 373 22775 2

46-0606

*Printed and bound in Spain
by Litografía Rosés S.A., Barcelona*

DOREEN ROBERTS

lives with her husband, who is also her manager and her biggest fan, in the beautiful city of Portland, Oregon. She believes that everyone should have a little adventure now and again to add interest to their lives. She believes in taking risks and has been known to embark on an adventure or two of her own. She is happiest, however, when she is creating stories about the biggest adventure of all—falling in love and learning to live happily ever after.

CAST OF CHARACTERS

Cully Black—The small-town sheriff thought he'd seen the last of Ginny Matthews. But now she's back and in trouble, and it's up to Cully to save her life—and maybe his own, as well.

Ginny Matthews—Ginny had never planned to return to Gold Peak. But when her former foster parents, Mabel and Jim Corbett, are brutally murdered, she's forced to face the past once more, as well as the deadly present.

Luke Sorenson—The scruffy, shifty quarryman was also a foster child of the Corbetts. He wanted something from them…badly enough to kill?

Old Man Wetherby—The aged, surly recluse always carries a shotgun. He's mean, he hates Jim Corbett, and he's out for revenge.

Sally Irwin—Bright and breezy barmaid Sally was Ginny's best friend in the old days. But this isn't the old days any more. Maybe Sally was just in the wrong place at the wrong time. Maybe.

David Petersen—Only Sally knows who he is and why he's in town. She might also know what he's up to, but if so, she's not talking.

My thanks to Sheriff Dave Daniel, Josephine County, Oregon, for your patience and for the valuable information. You were a great help.

And to Bill, who is my hero in every way, and who makes all things possible. Thank you.
I love you.

Chapter One

Sheriff Cully Black jammed his fists hard into the pockets of his black windcheater. Seventy feet below where he stood on a craggy bluff of the mountain, the twin beams from his deputies' flashlights probed the thick shadows of the night. They roamed across the wreckage of the familiar pickup, searching for signs of life.

Cully knew it was pointless. No one could have survived that crash. He tilted his chin high enough to see past the wide brim of his hat and stared bleakly at the stars scattered across the dark velvet sky. Maybe someone had borrowed the truck. Maybe it was someone else lying crushed behind the wheel.

It was a slim hope but he held on to it until Jed and Cory climbed back up the steep gully and reached the road, both of them panting from the exertion.

Cully braced himself. In the half-light of the waning moon he saw Jed's face. The deputy had trouble meeting his gaze.

"Sorry, Cully," he muttered. "Guess there's nothing we can do now."

Cully nodded, his lips clamped so tightly together

he could taste blood. When he could draw breath, he asked harshly, "Both of them?"

"Yep."

"You're sure?"

"Dead sure," Jed told him, with just a trace of irony.

"Okay. I'll wait for the medic." Cully checked his watch. "You two get back to bed. It'll be dawn in an hour or two."

"I'll wait with you." Jed tipped his hat back and scratched his head.

"Me, too," Cory muttered.

"He's gotta come out from Rapid City," Cully reminded them. "That's more than forty miles away." As if echoing his words, the thin wail of a siren floated across the mountainside on the wings of a strong breeze.

"Reckon that's him now," Jed said quietly.

Still unable to accept what had happened, Cully drew an unsteady breath. "You're sure. About down there, I mean."

Jed's face looked drawn in the ghostly moonlight. "Cully…"

Cully lifted his hand. "Okay. I just want to know, that's all."

He'd seen more than his share of death and destruction during his years in law enforcement. He was hardened by it, almost to the point of detachment. It was part of the job—a job he struggled to give his all.

The law and his horses. That was all he needed to make him happy. There was nothing better to keep his mind off the seamy side of life than taking a wild ride in the saddle under a western sky—head on into the clean, sharp winds that blew in from the mountains.

Right now he wished like hell that he was riding into that wind. Right now he didn't want to look death in the face. No matter how tough a skin he'd grown, it couldn't protect him now. Because down there, crushed inside what was left of the shattered pickup, lay the mangled bodies of two people who'd meant the world to him.

Normally his deputies wouldn't have called him out to the scene of an accident. They would have handled it themselves and made their report in the morning. It had been Jed who'd recognized the pickup and figured he'd want to know about it. Half-asleep, Cully had thrown on a pair of jeans and a sweatshirt, grabbed his jacket and leaped into his Jeep to hightail it out to Gold Peak.

Jim and Mabel Corbett weren't just friends and neighbors. They'd given him a home and stability when he'd needed it the most. They'd given him the chance to turn his life around and become a man.

"Cully?"

At the sound of Jed's worried voice, Cully lifted his hat and settled it more firmly on his head. The siren wailed again, much closer. "They're almost here," he said shortly. "I'm going down there to wait for them."

"I'll come, too."

Cully raised his hand. "No. Give me a moment alone with them." Without waiting for an answer he plunged, half-sliding, half-leaping, down the gully.

He had to hold his breath as he directed the beam

of his flashlight over the crumpled vehicle. Thank God it hadn't caught fire. He'd prepared himself for what he might see but when he caught sight of Jim's hand in a death grip on the wheel, his throat closed on him.

According to Jed, the call had come in more than an hour ago. A passing motorist had seen the headlights of the truck careening down the mountain road, then vanish. The witness had also reported the noise of the crash, echoing across the craggy peaks that had given the town its name.

Cully frowned. It was an odd time for Jim and Mabel to be going somewhere. The elderly couple rarely went out at night and usually went to bed after watching the local news at 10:00 p.m. For them to leave their house around two in the morning meant there had to be some kind of emergency.

He sat down on a small boulder and finally allowed himself to think beyond the stark details. Then, and only then, did he let the image of her into his mind.

Ginny.

This would break her heart.

It must have been twelve years since he'd last seen her, yet the very thought of her still jabbed at him like the sting of a scorpion.

She'd been barely nineteen back then. Tall and willowy, her dark hair flowing to her shoulders, her eyes blazing green fire, she'd faced him across the worn slats of the fence that bordered the Corbetts' house, hurling a tirade of words designed to hurt.

They'd hurt all right, though he'd never let her see that. It had been the toughest thing he'd ever had to do in his life but he'd let her go. It had seemed the right thing to do at the time. He'd spent the past twelve years or so trying to convince himself of that.

He'd died a little when she'd left and he'd died a little more when he'd heard she'd married. It was the last time Mabel had mentioned her name and he'd been too damn proud to ask after that.

Ginny should know about this. She'd want to know. If only he knew how to get in touch with her. Even Jim and Mabel didn't know where she was. Or so they'd said. Maybe they were just trying to save him from more heartache. In any case, it was too late now. The Corbetts were dead and he'd lost the last fragile connection to the woman he'd never been able to forget.

He sat there, head buried in his hands until the whine of the siren died above his head. He watched the medics work the best they could through the smashed windows of the truck. He wasn't surprised by the verdict. Both victims apparently had died instantly. They'd know more when they got the bodies out, which wouldn't be until the next day when they could get equipment down there to pry open the doors.

It wasn't until much later when alone in his car on his way back home, something else occurred to him. A tiny detail maybe but enough to spark the instincts that had always served him so well in the past.

The more he thought about it, the more convinced he became that something was very wrong with the whole picture. Something that didn't add up. He pressed his foot hard on the accelerator, knowing that now he wouldn't rest easy again until he'd figured out exactly what had happened in the last hours of the lives of Jim and Mabel Corbett.

THE PUNCH CAME at her hard and fast, aimed straight at her face. She ducked but wasn't quite quick enough. The cruel fist grazed her cheek, slamming her into the wall. Clutching her bruised shoulder, she faced the man advancing on her.

His contorted face was ugly with fury. He snarled at her, each word piercing her heart like lethal slivers of cold steel. *If you ever try to leave me, I'll hunt you down. I'll mess up that pretty face of yours so that no man will ever look at you without shuddering.*

He raised his hand, holding the pointed blade of the knife just inches from her face. Light glinted along the razor-sharp edge as he brought it closer. *You're mine, Virginia, and you'll be mine until the day we die. Longer, because if you have the guts to outlive me, I'll come right back to haunt you. You will never be rid of me. Never.*

She tried to call out for help, knowing that none was there. And then she was awake, his mocking laughter still ringing in her ears. Her lunging hand found the lamp and light flooded the room.

She sat up, hugged her knees and rocked until the perspiration on her forehead dried and her heart slowed to its normal beat. The nightmare was nothing new. She'd endured it over and over again.

But then, as the fog of sleep cleared, memory returned. Brandon was dead. Things had changed after all.

She had nothing to fear now. He could never hurt her again. She was finally free.

Or was she? Three months and still the nightmares persisted. Why couldn't she rid herself of the memories? Why couldn't she just forget the past, put it all behind her and get on with her life?

You will never be rid of me. Never.

Shuddering, she lay back down and pulled the covers over her bare shoulders. He was right. He may well be dead but he still haunted her dreams and tormented her mind. God help her.

Reluctant to go back to sleep, she finally crawled out of bed and wandered into the kitchen. The digital clock on the wall told her it was a little past 5:00 a.m. Coffee would be awfully good right now.

As the welcome fragrance filled the organized kitchen of her elegant town house, she made a determined effort to banish the last remnants of the nightmare. Even so, she couldn't shake the uneasy feeling that had persisted ever since last night.

At first, she hadn't been too concerned when her phone call a few nights ago had gone unanswered. She had simply assumed that Jim and Mabel were out visiting neighbors, or were enjoying a barn dance in the drafty, beat-up old barn on the Ridgewood Highway, a mile out of Gold Peak.

She filled her cup with steaming black coffee and carried it out to her living room. Sinking onto the sumptuous blue suede couch, she stretched out her legs and tried to still the tremors in her stomach.

When she'd called the next day and still the Corbetts didn't answer, the niggling worry had begun eating at her. She'd told herself that Jim was probably working in the yard, or fussing with the chickens. Mabel could be hanging out the wash, taking advantage of a stiff breeze to save electricity. Mabel was always looking for ways to save since Jim had retired.

But then she'd realized that the answering machine had been turned off. And that wasn't like Jim at all. He hated to miss out on anything. He made a point of stopping by the barber's at least once a week to catch up on the local gossip. He would never intentionally turn off the answering machine.

She'd tried to convince herself that the machine was broken and Jim was having it repaired. Or maybe waiting to buy a new one at Pitkin's general store. He might even have had to order one from a catalog, or drive into Rapid City to get one. Perhaps that's where he and Mabel had gone on a sunny afternoon. Shopping in Rapid City.

She'd waited two long days before trying to call again. Still no answer. And now the worry had become a nagging ache.

It had been many years since she'd last seen Mabel and Jim Corbett. When she'd finally found the courage to leave Brandon nine months ago, she'd changed her name and moved to the east coast. Fearing that he'd force her whereabouts from her former foster parents, she'd kept her new address and name a secret, even from them. When she called them, she used her cell phone. Brandon was devious. He had power. He had resources. She wouldn't be that tough to find.

After the news of his death, she'd thought about going back to Gold Peak to see Jim and Mabel. But the nightmares had been so invasive, so frightening, so realistic, she still hadn't been able to venture from her safe cocoon—the new life she'd created, where no one knew her history, or her real name.

She wasn't Ginny Matthews from Gold Peak, Oregon anymore. She wasn't Virginia Pierce, captive wife of Brandon Pierce. She was Justine Madison and for anyone who'd asked, she'd invented a family in California. The past twelve years had turned her into a city girl. She didn't belong in Gold Peak now.

Then again, maybe there had been another reason she didn't want to go back. A compelling reason in the shape of a six-foot-one, dark-haired cowboy by the name of Cully Black.

The moment his name popped into her mind she saw him, as clear as the day she'd told him she was leaving town for good. She'd searched his face that day, hoping in vain to see some kind of regret in his eyes. The color of charcoal, they'd stared back at her, cool and indifferent, killing all hopes she'd ever raised.

He'd seemed so distant, so unapproachable, it was hard to believe they'd ever slept in each other's arms after a reckless night of lovemaking—a night of crazy passion she'd never known before or since. No, the last person in the world she wanted to see again was Cully.

Even so, she was worried about her former foster parents. For some reason, the urge to see them, talk to them, was overwhelming. Maybe she could talk them into flying to Philadelphia. She could show them the city, take them to see Independence Hall, the Liberty Bell, The Franklin Institute. Buy them a cheesesteak. Jim would love that. And Mabel would adore

Liberty Place, with its myriad shops and ethnic food outlets.

Excited at the prospect, she glanced at the pendulum clock on her mantelpiece. It was two-thirty in the morning in Oregon. She would have to call when she got home from work. Her invitation would just have to wait.

CULLY HAD WAITED all day for the coroner's report. It came just as he'd locked the door of his office behind him and was halfway down the steps to the street.

He was looking forward to getting home. Nothing eased the stress of a hard day faster than the snuffling sounds of welcome his horses gave him when he walked into his stables. Their earthy smell, their rough hair beneath his fingers, the nudge of a cold nose against his cheek, all of it was his reward for having made it through another day.

Soon after he'd been elected sheriff, he'd bought the modest horse ranch in the hopes of escaping some of the pressure and the pain that haunted him. Having practically grown up in the small town buried at the foot of Oregon's Eastern mountains, he'd been around horses most of his life.

Next to his dedication to upholding the law, horses were his greatest passion. There were times when dealing with the tragic side of life weighed heavily on his mind. Particularly the last two days. His horses helped lighten the load. Considerably. Mabel had been right when she'd told him he'd always be a cowboy at heart.

When his cell phone jingled he reached for it, hoping it wasn't another call that would take him away from his supper. Lyla Whittaker, his housekeeper, usually stayed long enough to serve him up a hot meal, unless he was late getting home. Those nights he had to make do with warming something up in the microwave. He wasn't in the mood for the microwave tonight.

He answered the phone with a curt, "Sheriff Black."

It was the coroner and he listened intently as the mild voice told him what he'd suspected all along. "Looks like they'd been dead about an hour or so before the crash. Guess you got a crime on your hands, Cully."

"Sure looks that way." Cully briefly closed his eyes. Who in hell would want to hurt two of the most generous, neighborly people he'd ever known? It had to be a robbery. Not that the Corbetts had much to steal. They'd always lived a frugal life, not being ones to buy fancy cars or boats and the like. He couldn't even remember them ever taking a vacation away from home. They'd given their lives to their foster kids, until they'd gotten too old to keep up with the work.

He thanked the coroner and shoved his phone back in his pocket. First thing in the morning he'd apply for a warrant to go over the house. Take a look around. It was as good a place as any to start.

In a hurry to get home now, he swung himself into his Jeep and started the engine. As far as he knew, the Corbetts had no family. No kids, no relatives to notify. Unless he found something in his search of their home that told him different. Maybe he'd find something that would tell him where Ginny had disappeared to. She needed to know what had happened. Too bad she'd miss the funeral in the morning. She would have wanted to be there.

He tried to ignore the faint twinge of anticipation. It wouldn't do to go getting any ideas about her. She was married now. He didn't even know her married name, so it wasn't likely he'd be able to track her down. In any case, she'd let him know long ago how she felt about him. Even if he found her, he sure as hell wasn't giving her the chance to tell him all over again.

THE FOLLOWING EVENING Ginny stood in the quiet luxury of her living room, the phone pressed anxiously against her ear. She'd promised herself that if she got no answer this time, she'd call the police and have them check out the Corbetts' home. She would have done it last night, except that in Gold Peak the police meant the county sheriff and that meant Cully Black.

Outside her window, the sultry Philadelphia heat shimmered on the cars parked in the parking lot. Kids ran barefoot in and out of the vehicles, their shouts muffled by the thick glass. Everything seemed so normal, yet her heart pounded unevenly as she waited, praying to hear Jim's gruff voice on the other end of the line.

Unbelievably, the line clicked open. Her gasp of relief echoed in her ears as she said breathlessly, "Jim? Where have you *been?* I've been so worried, I—"

Shock slammed into her as the deep voice answered her. A voice quite different from Jim's harsh tones. A voice that she recognized, even after all these years. "Ma'am? This is Sheriff Cully Black. I'm afraid Jim's not here."

For what seemed like an eternity she struggled to get her breath. She needed to steady her voice, not to let him know he could still affect her. She waited so long he spoke again.

"Ma'am?" Then his voice changed, dropping even lower. "*Ginny?* Is that you?"

It had been so long since anyone had called her by that name. For just a second or two, she felt a tug of sweet nostalgia, until she remembered the last day she'd seen him. The day he'd shattered her dreams.

Instinct urged her to hang up but then Mabel's sweet face swam into her mind and she swallowed.

Her fingers gripped the phone so hard she felt them cramp. The three thousand miles between them melted away and she felt as if he were right there in the room with her. She loosened her grip and struggled to keep her voice as casual as possible. "What are you doing there, Cully? Where's Jim?" A rush of alarm tightened her nerves. "There's nothing wrong with him, is there? Is Mabel there?"

"Ginny…"

She heard something else in his voice then and the chill spread rapidly throughout her body. For some idiotic reason she didn't want to hear what he had to say and went on talking as if he hadn't said her name in that awful tone that smacked of sympathy and sorrow. "Their answering machine doesn't seem to be working and I was worried…"

"Ginny, listen to me."

She pressed a hand over her mouth as she heard him say the unbelievable words. *Mabel and Jim died in a car wreck on the mountain, both dead, funeral was yesterday.*

"No-o-o-o-o!" The hollow cry echoed around her living room, bounced off the colorless walls and beat mercilessly back into her ears. Vaguely she heard Cully's voice repeating her name over and over but nothing made sense. Nothing. They couldn't be dead. It had to be a mistake.

"Ginny, please, don't hang up."

Cully's urgent voice finally penetrated the loud humming in her head. Holding back a sob, she whispered, "How did it happen?"

"We don't know." He sounded ragged, weary, as if he hadn't slept in days. He'd always had a huskiness in his voice—a sexy rawness that had once thrilled her to the core. But it was more pronounced now, as if every word he spoke were painful. "It was late at night. You know how that road winds down the mountain. It was dark, not much moonlight…"

She couldn't take any more. "I have to go. I can't…"

"Ginny, don't hang up! *Don't!*"

The urgency in his words frightened her. "I'm sorry." She gulped, afraid she was going to bawl right there into the phone. "I know it must be hard for you, too. But right now I don't feel much like talking."

"Wait, I've been trying to find you."

His pause seemed fraught with tension. She gripped the phone, prepared to stand her ground if he asked her to come home. There was no point now.

"Ginny, the will is being read in two days. You need to be there."

She shook her head at him, even though he couldn't see her. "No, I don't see why. I'm not a relative."

"Paul Bellman, he's the Corbetts' lawyer now. He needs you there."

She swallowed. "Did he say why?"

"No, he didn't."

Her mind raced with questions. She couldn't be a beneficiary. The Corbetts had been her foster parents, as they had to dozens of kids in their lifetime. As far as she knew they had nothing to leave, anyway.

"Ginny? Come home. You should be here. At least give me a number where I can reach you."

Her instincts, honed by months of hiding in the shadows, bunched into a solid wall. "No, I don't think that's a good idea."

She felt sick, still unable to believe that the only real parents she had known were gone. Yet somewhere in there, she felt guilt, as well. She had never had the chance to say goodbye. The least she could do was visit their graves and say her goodbyes there. It would give her closure, if nothing else.

Before she could change her mind again, she said sharply, "Never mind. I'll come home. I'll be there tomorrow." She hung up then and gave herself up to the awful, tearing sobs of grief.

THREE THOUSAND miles away, Cully let the receiver fall gently onto its rest. He should have told her all of it. He just hadn't been able to bring himself to hurt her even more than she was already.

This way he could give her a little time to get over

the shock, before she found out that the Corbetts hadn't died in an accident after all. Before he had to tell her that the couple she had loved as parents had been brutally murdered.

Chapter Two

It was late afternoon, the following day, when Ginny drove the white Taurus she'd rented into Gold Peak. There was only one motel in that whole miserable town and it was the last place on earth she wanted to stay. The motel had been built before she was born and the ancient, decaying building she remembered had not improved with time.

She'd thought about staying in Rapid City, which at least boasted a halfway decent hotel but that meant driving the extra forty miles back to town and she was already exhausted. A sleepless night and the scramble to get on a plane early that morning had taken its toll.

All the rooms had outside doors that faced onto the parking lot and the only way to reach the upper floor was by a weather-beaten flight of stairs. Rather than walk up those creaking steps, she asked for a room on the ground floor.

The room, as it turned out, wasn't quite as bad as she'd feared. The bedding, though shabby, looked reasonably clean and the plumbing at least seemed to be working. The seascape hanging above the headboard looked out of place—a poor attempt to make the room less forbidding. It failed miserably.

Reminding herself that it was only for one night, she took a quick, refreshing shower and changed into shorts and a T-shirt.

Seated on the edge of the bed, she studied the phone for a long time before finally reaching for it. After stabbing out Cully's number, she waited, heart thumping unevenly, for him to answer.

His voice sounded wary when he answered, as if he'd known it would be her calling.

She spoke quickly, afraid her raw emotion would be misinterpreted. "Cully? This is Ginny. I'm at the Sagebrush Motel. I just got into town. I need to talk to you. Is now a good time?"

A slight pause, then his voice, deeper now, drawled in her ear again. "It's almost suppertime. How about I meet you at the Red Steer in a half hour? We can get a bite to eat and talk there."

She'd deliberately held the memories at bay as she'd driven into town. There were things she didn't want to remember about her life in Gold Peak. But at the mention of the Red Steer tavern, the past surged back into her mind just as sharp and as painful as if it were just a few days ago.

It was there at the Red Steer when she'd first stepped into Cully's arms. He'd asked her to dance and, egged on by Sally Irwin, her best friend, she'd accepted the challenge in Cully's dark eyes. The moment his arms had closed around her, she'd known that nothing would ever be the same again.

"Ginny?"

She jumped and answered quickly. "I don't want to take up too much of your time. I just have a couple of questions, that's all. I plan on visiting the graves, then getting to bed early. I have to drive back to the airport tomorrow."

"You gotta eat, don't you?"

"Well, yes, but I thought a pizza in my room…"

"The steak's still real good at the Red Steer. You always enjoyed a good steak. Besides, there's something I need to tell you."

"Can't you tell me on the phone?"

"I think it's better if we discuss it in person. Over that steak and a cold beer."

She struggled with indecision, torn between the tantalizing prospect of a wonderful steak dinner and her deep reluctance to face Cully again. She hadn't planned on meeting him in person. If it hadn't been for something that had occurred to her late last night and had been bothering her all day, she wouldn't even have called him.

Then again, she was hungry. The airline food had been skimpy and unpalatable. And maybe what she needed to ask him was better done in person after all. "I'll be there in half an hour."

She replaced the receiver, instantly regretting the impulse. Her mind in a whirl, she rummaged in her bag for the jeans she'd planned to wear on the plane the next day. After a lengthy debate with herself, she decided not to change the T-shirt. A dash of lipstick, a flick of the comb and she was ready. As ready as she was ever going to be, she thought ruefully.

A few minutes later she drove out of the motel

parking lot, followed by a grimy minivan. Its dark tinted windows made it difficult to see who drove it. She slowed to let it pass but it kept pace behind her, following her for the three miles to the tavern. Not surprising really, since there was only one road into town.

Even so, the long months she'd spent hiding in the shadows had kept her constantly on guard, to the point where the most mundane thing could seem threatening.

Driving down Main Street, she credited her shivery uneasiness to the memories that jarred her mind. The first time she'd stood, drained of emotion, in the huge living room of Mabel and Jim Corbett's old house. The confusion of sharing her life with a dozen or so kids, all hurting inside like her, all afraid to trust.

Cully had been one of those kids. Older than her by ten years, he'd left by the time she was nine. But if it hadn't been for Cully, she never would have survived that first year in the foster home. She blinked hard, determined not to give in to the past. She'd left it all behind a long time ago. Too long ago.

She parked in a familiar spot outside the Red Steer, noting with an absurd sense of relief that the minivan had passed on by. No matter how often she reminded herself that she no longer had anything to fear, it was tough to let go of the constant apprehension, the mistrust of anything unfamiliar.

Her heart skipped when she saw the red Jeep Cherokee parked close to the entrance. It had to belong to Cully. He'd always been partial to red. She'd hoped to get there ahead of him—give herself time to reacquaint herself with the place before she had to deal with him.

Every muscle in her body felt tight as she pushed through the swing doors that led into the dining room. The orange lamps, fastened to the walls in their wrought iron cages, were turned down low. The huge brick fireplace still dominated the room and in spite of the warmth outside, a crackling log fire spit flames up the massive chimney.

She saw him at once. He was seated with his back to a window, facing the door as if he'd been watching for her. She pulled in a deep breath and walked unsteadily across the room, wishing like hell she'd listened to her instincts and ordered that pizza.

Cully rose to his feet as she approached, his expression unreadable. He looked older, she noticed, and remembered with a shock that he was now forty-one years old. Deep creases etched the corners of his eyes. His hair, still springy and dark, showed no sign of gray, except for just above his ears at the temples.

He'd filled out from the tall, lanky cowboy she remembered. His denim shirt stretched across a broad chest and beneath the rolled-up sleeves his upper arms were solid muscle. He wore the hard, tough look of a man who spent most of his days weathering the harsh environment of the mountains. It looked good on him. Too good.

She reached the table and hesitated, wondering if she should shake hands or just sit down in the chair he'd pulled out. "It's good to see you, Cully." Even to her ears, her voice sounded stilted, almost hostile.

Something flickered in his eyes, then he held out his hand. "You, too."

She watched her fingers briefly disappear in his warm, sunburned grip, then he let her go. His hand had felt strong, secure. It had been a mistake to come. She sat down, trying to figure out a way to get out of this gracefully.

"I've ordered the steaks," Cully said, taking away her options. "I hope you still like 'em medium rare."

She nodded and slid her gaze away from the appraisal in his eyes. She must look older, too. God knows she felt every one of her thirty one years.

"You look real good, Ginny."

She started, remembering his uncanny ability to read her mind. From the first moment he'd set eyes on her, he seemed to know what she was thinking, even before she did.

"I'm not Ginny anymore," she said quietly. "My name is Justine now."

His answer unsettled her even more. "It makes no difference what fancy name you've given yourself. You'll always be Ginny to me."

He'd teased her that first day, telling her it would be her job to milk the cows at the crack of dawn every morning. Then he'd patted her shoulder and promised he'd watch out for her. *You don't have to be afraid of nothing as long as I'm around,* he'd said. *Them cows are more afraid of you than you are of them. You just holler at 'em and watch 'em run.*

Grateful for his understanding, for the first time since arriving at that rambling old farmhouse, she'd smiled. He'd seemed so tall, so powerful. She remembered looking way up into his dark gray eyes and knowing somehow that here was someone she could trust.

From then on she'd followed him around like Mary's little lamb, until a short year later when he'd gone to help out on the Double K Ranch. The home she'd come to love had seemed empty after he'd gone.

She made herself push the memories away.

He sat twisting the mug of beer in front of him between his strong fingers, not looking at her. "I'm real sorry you had to come back to this. I know how you felt about Mabel and Jim. It must have hurt bad to hear what happened."

She made an effort to control the wobble in her voice. "I still can't believe it happened. Jim was such a careful driver."

Something in his face changed and he glanced over at the bar. "Get you a beer?"

"I don't drink beer anymore. A glass of white wine would be good, though."

The corner of his mouth lifted in a cynical smile. "Oh, right. I forgot. City gals don't drink beer."

It shouldn't have hurt. She wasn't sure why it did. On the defensive, she said crisply, "We city folk tend to be civilized."

"Is that what they're calling it nowadays?" He shoved his chair back, scraping the feet on the hardwood floor. "I'll be right back."

She watched him get up and head for the bar. She wasn't surprised to hear he'd gone into law enforcement. He'd once told her that he'd run away from home when he was a kid and a friendly cop had found him a place in the Corbett household. He'd talked a lot about being a cop.

Mabel had told her that he'd left the ranch and gone to Rapid City for training. That was right after she'd turned her back on the town for good. It hadn't taken him long to be assigned as deputy in McKewen County and eventually located in Gold Peak. She might have known he'd end up back here.

He came back with her wine and set it in front of her. She murmured her thanks and waited for him to sit down.

Before she could ask what she wanted to know, he said casually, "Paul's reading the will at ten o'clock tomorrow morning at his office. I'll pick you up at the motel and run you over there."

She gave a decisive shake of her head. "Sorry, I'm booked to fly back on the midday flight. I have to be back at work the next day."

He drained the last of his beer. "They can't do without you for a couple of days?"

She almost smiled. "No, they can't."

"Must be a tough job if you're so indispensable."

"It's a responsible one. I'm head fashion buyer for a well-known department store. I'm supposed to be ordering for the spring line and the samples will be coming in any day now." She sent him a cynical look from under her lashes. "I don't expect you to understand."

If he was stung by the remark, he showed no sign of it. "Paul was pretty insistent you be there. He's been trying to get ahold of you. No one knew where you were. Not even Mabel or Jim. I didn't even know you were in touch with them until you called yesterday.''

She dropped her gaze and fiddled with the stem of her wineglass. "I can't imagine why their lawyer would need me there."

Cully shrugged. "Maybe he wants you to take care of their personal effects. What with Jim or Mabel not having any family and all, someone needs to clear out the house before it's sold. Though I think Paul has a list of things they wanted to leave to some of the kids."

For a long time she stared at her glass, struggling with indecision. Then she said wearily, "I suppose I could talk to him. I really hadn't planned on staying that long."

"So you said."

Ignoring the irony in his voice she said sharply, "There's something I don't understand about the accident. You said it happened late at night?"

"Yep." He reached for his second beer and she had the feeling he was deliberately avoiding her gaze.

"How late?"

He shrugged and answered reluctantly, "Around two in the morning."

"And Jim was driving?"

He swallowed several mouthfuls of the golden liquid then slowly set the glass mug down in front of him. "He was behind the wheel when the truck crashed."

She knew him well enough to know when he was keeping something from her. Her hand trembled as she lifted her glass. She let the mellow wine slide down her throat, then said carefully, "Cully, you know as well as I do that Jim never drove at night. He had night blindness. They rarely went out at night, certainly never that late and if they did, Mabel always drove."

The silence between them stretched into minutes, while a nasal voice from the speakers, accompanied by guitars, sang about a mangled heart.

Finally Cully sighed. "I know. I had the same thought. Which is why I had the wreck investigated. I guess this is as good a time as any to tell you. I figured you wouldn't want to be alone when you heard. It wasn't an accident, Ginny. Jim and Mabel were already dead when the truck went off the road. I'm real sorry."

Her breath seemed to be caught somewhere in her throat. This was worse than anything she could have imagined. For some silly reason, it was on the tip of her tongue to remind him her name wasn't Ginny anymore. Except it didn't seem to matter now. She'd always been Ginny in her heart, no matter how hard she'd tried to escape the past.

She made her lips move. "What happened?"

"They'd both been shot at close range. We think by Jim's shotgun, which is missing. Could have been a burglary that went bad, though there was no sign of a break-in. Then again, it could have been a drifter looking for a handout. Knowing Jim and Mabel, they might have invited him in for a meal and things got ugly. The house looked like a tornado had gone through it. Lamps smashed, chairs overturned, drawers pulled out of dressers…a real mess.''

She shuddered. ''And you have no idea who it was?''

''Not yet.'' His mouth tightened in a grim line. ''But I will.'' For a long moment he kept his gaze on his hands then slowly, he raised his chin.

Her twinge of awareness took her by surprise. She felt as she had that first time, the little kid in awe of the big, bold cowboy. She hadn't expected to be still affected by him like this. If she had, she would have refused his invitation. She made herself look into his eyes and saw nothing there but concern.

''Look,'' he said softly, ''I know all this is a shock to you and that you'll need some time to deal with it. But I could use your help. You probably remember better than I do what the Corbetts had in their home. I need you to take a look and see if you can figure out if there's anything missing. It might help catch the bastard who did this.''

Still dazed, she muttered, ''I don't understand how anyone could hurt Mabel and Jim.''

''I know,'' Cully said grimly. ''I have a bad feeling about this. A feeling somehow that this isn't the end of it.''

His words made the back of her neck prickle. At that precise moment, a shadow appeared at the window behind him. She hadn't been directly looking in that direction and by the time she did, whoever it was had disappeared. It was more an impression than anything but something about that fleeting silhouette disturbed her.

She shook her head, impatient with her erratic mind. Cully's words had put her on edge, making her imagine things that weren't there. The very idea of someone killing Jim and Mabel shocked and sickened her. No wonder she was feeling jittery. She couldn't imagine why anyone would want to harm such generous, giving people as the Corbetts, people who just about everyone in Gold Peak had known and loved.

The steaks arrived, brought to the table by a young man with a scruffy stubble darkening his jaw and a plaited gold ring in his right ear. He stared hard at Ginny as he set down the plates.

"This is Luke Sorensen." Cully waved his hand at the frankly curious man. "He helps out on Sally's night off. He lived with the Corbetts for a while, right Luke? Meet another one of the Corbetts' foster kids. Ginny Matthews."

"My name's not…" she began, then shrugged her tired shoulders. It didn't matter anymore. Brandon was dead. It didn't matter what people called her now.

She shook the reluctant hand Luke held out. "I was so sad to hear about the Corbetts' deaths. I wish I could have been at the funeral."

"Yeah, it was bad news," Luke muttered. He dropped his hand and slunk back to the bar.

Ginny frowned at Cully. "You said something about Sally. You don't mean Sally Irwin, do you?"

Cully picked up his steak knife. "Yeah, that's our Sally. Oh, right, I forgot. You two used to be pretty good buddies."

"Best friends." She stared at the thick steak on her

plate, wondering how on earth she was going to eat anything at all. "We lost touch over the years."

"Yeah, city life will do that to you."

Deciding to ignore the sarcasm in his voice, she tackled the steak, realizing all of a sudden that she was starving.

Across the table, Cully watched her out of the corner of his eye. She'd changed. It shocked him how much she'd changed. It wasn't so much the hair, cut short and lighter than he remembered. It wasn't even that she was older. She didn't look that much older than the day she'd left town to move to Phoenix. The Arizona sun had given her a few faint lines here and there but she still had that fresh, clear skin. In the tight jeans and T-shirt she wore her body looked just as firm and as slender as the night he'd covered her with his naked body and taken them both to another world.

Angry about his obsession with the past, he concentrated on the present. She'd become citified. Even the jeans couldn't hide that air of sophistication that set them worlds apart. She looked out of place, like a tourist trying to blend in somewhere she didn't belong.

It was more than that, though. There was something else. It was in her eyes. That unforgettable blend of green and gold still reminded him of cool forests and sunlit waterfalls but there was a look in them that worried him.

He'd seen that look before, in the eyes of a bruised and battered woman he'd pulled out of busted-up trailer after arresting her raging, drunken husband. The look of the hunted. The terrified. The victim.

He swallowed a bite of steak then asked abruptly, "How come your husband didn't come with you?"

He saw the expression he dreaded in her face—the flicker of fear, the tightening of her jaw. Then she said something he hadn't expected.

Her words were flat, as if she were making a conscious effort to erase all emotion from her voice. "My husband's dead. He was killed in a plane crash three months ago."

He choked, grabbed his beer and took a huge gulp. "I'm sorry. Thank God you weren't with him."

She sawed at her steak, her face a cold, hard mask. "Yes," she said deliberately. "Thank God."

Something about the way she said it put a chill right through his bones. "That must have been real tough," he said awkwardly.

Carefully, she lifted a small, neat square of meat to her mouth, chewed it and swallowed. "I'm sorry I missed Sally. I would have enjoyed talking to her."

His mouth twisted. So she didn't want to talk about it. Well, okay. It was none of his business anyway.

He shouldn't feel so damn pleased about it. It wasn't right to feel glad a man had died. Maybe he wouldn't if he didn't have a gut feeling that her marriage hadn't exactly been made in paradise. Then again, if he were really honest with himself, the news that she was no longer married wasn't going to upset him too much, no matter how happy or miserable she'd been.

Still feeling guilty about his lack of sympathy for

the dead man, he accepted her switch in the conversation. For the next half hour or so he caught her up to date on various people she'd known when she'd lived in Gold Peak.

She was sipping at a steaming cup of coffee when she brought up the subject of the Corbetts' deaths again. "I assume you've searched the house," she said, placing her mug carefully on the table.

"Yep. Judging by the way the place was messed up, Jim put up a pretty good fight. He didn't go down easy." He swallowed hard. "We think Mabel was killed in the hallway. Looks like she was trying to make a run for it when he caught up with her."

She shuddered, her face pale. "Didn't you find anything that might help find out who killed them?"

"So far we've got nothing to go on. Without a motive it's hard to know where to start." He thought about getting another beer, then decided against it. "The worst part is knowing that maniac is still running around out there. I need to stop him before he gets his hands bloody again."

She seemed to think about it for a long moment or two, then said quietly, "You're right. He has to pay for what he did. I'm not sure how much help I can be but I'll take a look at the house if you think it will help."

It wasn't until he relaxed his muscles that he realized just how tense he'd been. "Thanks, Ginny. I sure appreciate your cooperation."

Her face was bleak when she nodded. "I guess I can stop by to see the Corbetts' lawyer, then I'll go with you to the house."

"Great. I'll pick you up at eight-forty-five."

"I have a car. I'll find it."

"I have to be there, too. I might as well pick you up."

Her indifferent shrug stung his pride. "If you like."

She reached for her purse and he said quickly, "I'll take care of it."

She gave him a tight smile. "Thanks. You were right. The steaks are still good here."

"My pleasure, ma'am." He pushed his chair back. "Can I give you a ride back to the Sagebrush?"

She stood with him, avoiding his gaze. "Thanks, but I have my car. I'll see you tomorrow."

He watched her leave, cursing the ache under his ribs. He knew better than to let his emotions get the better of him. She was even more out of his reach now than she'd been twelve years ago, when he'd watched her march away from him and out of his life.

She'd taken his heart with her that day and she'd cared so little about him it had taken her exactly ten months to forget him and find someone else to fall in love with. Ten months, while he'd waited and hoped. What a damn fool he'd been.

He picked up his hat and jammed it on his head. Well, there would be polar bears roaming the desert before he let anyone make an ass out of him again. He turned his back on the table and headed for the door.

GINNY CLIMBED into her car and gunned the engine. She was exhausted and wanted nothing more than to go back to the motel and fall into bed. She couldn't do that just yet. She couldn't go to sleep in this town without having visited the graves of the people who meant the world to her. She couldn't rest easy until she'd said her goodbyes. She deeply regretted having missed the funeral. This was all she had left. This last final farewell over their graves.

Cully had told her the Corbetts were buried in the cemetery on the hill. It was a beautiful spot, shaded by cottonwood trees, with a clear view of the mountain range in the west, where the sun had already dipped below the peaks.

In the shaded light of dusk the haphazard rows of gravestones rose and fell like undulating waves of a silent ocean. Her sneakers made hardly a sound on the pathway as she hurried past bouquets of roses and lilies of the valley, their sweet fragrance blending with the pungent smell of the pines.

She found the graves, freshly dug and with a gleaming white headstone with both their names carved on it. The coarse grass felt prickly beneath her knees but she knelt for a long time, allowing the bittersweet memories to take her back to a happier, carefree time, when she was loved and protected and safe from the world.

The darkness settled around her and the rustling of night creatures whispered among the trees, disturbing her thoughts. A cool breeze wafted a lock of her hair across her forehead and sighing, she climbed wearily to her feet. "Goodbye, Jim," she whispered. "Goodbye, Mabel. Thank you for the love you gave me and for the ten years of happiness I'll never forget." A sob choked her words and she struggled for a moment, striving to control her grief.

In the silence she thought she heard Jim's voice, whispering urgently in her ear. The words weren't clear to her but the message was.

"Cully will find out who did this to you," she said, her voice loud in the darkness. "I promise you both that Cully will hunt him down and see that he pays. No matter what it takes. Then you'll both be able to rest in peace."

The whispering stopped, bringing her the first small measure of peace she'd felt since hearing Cully's voice utter the inconceivable. With an ache in her heart she headed back to where she'd left the car.

The night had drawn in now, with only a tiny sliver of moon in the starlit sky to light the way. Below her she could see the lights of the little town, glowing like the embers of a dying fire. She shivered in the desert breeze that had suddenly grown cool.

She had neared the end of the path when without warning the shadow of a man crossed in front of her. For a startling second he was illuminated between her and the flickering lights below. Then, almost at once, he vanished.

Feeling cold and shaken, she assured herself her eyes were playing tricks with her. A deserted graveyard at night was no place to hang around on her own. No wonder she was seeing things.

She started walking…faster…and then she heard them. Distinct footsteps, echoing from behind her, keeping in time with her own.

Heart pounding in her throat she spun around, her

gaze probing the shadows for a sign of movement. The footsteps had stopped, too. All she could see were the branches of the cottonwoods swaying gently in the night wind.

She started off again, running now. There they were again...the footsteps...running with her, closer than before. A man's voice, low and guttural, laughing softly, the sound barely audible above the pounding of feet.

The terror gripped her like hands of steel, closing around her lungs, making it hard to breathe. Only a few more yards to go. Could she make it? Her legs were already trembling and weak. She had to make it, for she knew as sure as she knew her own name, that if those footsteps caught up with her, she'd end up just like Mabel and Jim, buried deep in the dark, cold ground.

Chapter Three

Reaching the car, Ginny fumbled in her purse for her keys. Her hand shook so badly she couldn't fit the key into the lock. He had to be right behind her. He had to be....

With a sob of relief she got the door open and slid inside. It was then that she realized the footsteps were no longer echoing out of the darkness. She slammed the door and locked it, then struggled to fit the key into the ignition. The engine fired and the beams from her headlights poured a wide swath of yellow light across the road ahead of her.

As she pulled out onto the road, she glanced into the rearview mirror, fully expecting to see her pursuer standing there, watching her leave.

There was no one there. No man, no other car, no lights, no movement, nothing. Had she imagined it? But she'd heard the footsteps, the ugly, taunting laugh...hadn't she?

The thought that the whole thing could have been nothing more than a wild flight of fancy terrified her almost as much as the reality of a stalker. For weeks now she'd been afraid that the long months of hiding had taken their toll and that she was losing her mind. It was getting to the point where she couldn't be sure anymore what was real and what was in her imagination.

Thoroughly shaken, she drove too fast, taking the curves down the hill at a speed that rocked the car from side to side. She couldn't outrun the cold feeling of dread that gripped her. Taking a long, deep breath, she made herself slow down. She wouldn't be much help to Cully if she landed in hospital.

Cully. Her mouth curved in a wry smile. What would he think of her if he knew the turmoil going on inside her? If he saw her fleeing from a monster that existed only in her troubled mind?

She'd always been so strong, so sure of who she was and what she wanted. The night she told him she had to get out of Gold Peak or she'd suffocate, he hadn't even tried to change her mind. He'd known it was useless. Once Ginny Matthews had her sights set on something, she didn't let go.

The trouble was, she didn't want to let go of him, either. She'd asked him to go with her. He'd told her in no uncertain terms that he wasn't city folk.

She could still hear his voice, harsh with bitterness, as he'd paced back and forth across the dingy living room of the apartment he'd rented above Bailey's Garage. "I lived in a city once. I know what it's like. People don't care a damn about each other. They'd watch their neighbor die on the street without lifting a finger to help."

"They can't all be like that."

"Well, they are. Take my word for it. It's a whole different world out there. There's a thief hanging around every dark corner and con artists just waiting to clean you out of your life savings. Folks trample all over each other to get their hands on stuff they don't need or want and all they care about is making more and more money. If that's what you want to be like, well you're welcome to it.''

"I don't have to be like them. I'm who I am. No one's going to change me."

"Believe me. The city changes everybody."

She'd been close to tears, angry at him for bursting her rosy bubble. "You'll never understand. I need to make something of my life. I don't want see it waste away in this boring little backwoods town."

"This boring little backwoods town was good enough for you when you were a kid looking for a home."

"Well, I'm not a kid anymore. I've grown up. And you're jealous because you don't have the guts to leave town. I'll be in Phoenix, making a new life for myself, while you're stuck here day after day mucking out Judd Taylor's stables. And you know what, Cully Black? It's no more than you deserve."

Maybe, if he'd begged her to stay, convinced her that he loved her as passionately as she loved him, she might have stayed in Gold Peak. She might have borne his babies and been content to make a home for them all.

But he hadn't said a word about love. He'd stood looking out through the dust-grimed window, his back as stiff and straight as a flagpole and his thumbs jammed into the pockets of his jeans.

She'd seen him only once more after that night. He'd stopped by the Corbetts' house, a couple of days before she planned to catch the bus out of town. At first, dizzy with hope, she'd thought he'd come to tell her he loved her and wanted her to stay. When she found out he'd stopped by to return a couple of books he'd borrowed from Jim, she'd finally faced the truth. She was good enough to lie in his bed but she wasn't good enough to share his life. Same old story.

She'd caught up with him as he was leaving and told him goodbye. Keeping the fence between them, she'd let all her pain out in a stream of accusations and criticism. He hadn't even flinched. That was how little he'd cared.

The blaze of lights from an oncoming car lit up her windshield, dazzling her. Realizing that her eyes were filled with tears, she dashed them away with the back of her hand. She'd done crying over Cully Black a long time ago. If she had any sense at all, she'd get right back on that plane tomorrow at noon and turn her back on Gold Peak forever.

She pulled into the parking lot of the Sagebrush Motel and cut the engine. Trouble was, she never did have any sense where Cully was concerned. It wasn't until she married Brandon that she realized what she'd truly lost.

Wearily she climbed out of the car and slammed the door. To hell with Cully Black. She'd talk to the lawyer in the morning and then go straight back to the airport. It had been too many years since she was in the Corbetts' house. How was she going to remember what they had enough to know it was missing?

Her sneakers made only a slight scuffling sound on the hard ground and she caught herself listening for the sound of echoing footsteps. Angry with herself, she closed the door of her room hard behind her. This is what Brandon had done to her. Turned her into a quivering mass of nerves.

If she didn't get it together, she'd start messing up at work and that could spell disaster. The board members of Whitman's Department Store had no patience with incompetent personnel.

She had her hand on the bathroom door when the harsh jangle of the phone made her jump. Frowning, she moved to answer it. She hadn't told anyone where she was staying, since she'd be there just for one night. The only person who knew she was there was Cully.

Her hand trembled as she lifted the receiver and muttered a cautious, "Hello?"

She waited for an answer that never came. The silence on the end of the line unnerved her and she repeated, louder this time, "Hello? Cully, is that you? Who *is* this?"

The room seemed to be closing in around her. Hastily she dropped the receiver onto its stand. It must have been a wrong number. Or one of those automatic sales calls that didn't go through. Anything. After all, she didn't hear any heavy breathing. It was nothing.

Even so, she found it hard to fall asleep. She kept hearing unfamiliar noises and her body tensed with every sound. After watching a meaningless movie on TV, she turned on the radio, buried her face beneath the sheet and concentrated on visions of quiet lakes and soothing waves breaking on a sandy shore.

She awoke in the middle of the night, heart thumping, a sheen of sweat prickling on her forehead. Unsure of what had disturbed her sleep, she lay awake for an hour or more, before falling once more into a fitful sleep. When she woke up again, sunlight filtered through the gap where the cheap curtains didn't quite meet.

A quick glance at the clock radio told her she'd slept later than she'd planned. Thankful that the nightmare had stayed away, she showered and pulled on the jeans she'd worn the night before. Her sleeveless blue shirt was the last clean item she had left. She packed the rest in a plastic laundry bag and stuffed it into her garment bag, then gathered up her stuff from the bathroom.

She had just finished checking out when Cully's Jeep pulled into the parking lot a little later. She watched through the window as he climbed out and headed for the door, his hat pulled down low to shade his eyes. She'd forgotten how good he looked in a cowboy hat.

Hastily, she pulled her gaze away from him and pretended to be studying a faded map on the wall when she heard him come through the door.

Her skin tingled as he came up behind her, his deep voice penetrating every nerve in her body. "Morning! Hope I didn't keep you waiting."

She plastered a smile on her face before turning to greet him. "Not at all. I've just checked out."

She thought she saw a shadow cross his face. His mouth tightened just a fraction. "Have you had breakfast yet?"

"Coffee and a bagel. In the coffee shop next door."

He gave her a brief nod. "Then I guess we're ready to go."

She squared her shoulders. "I'll follow you in my car. Then I can go straight to the airport after I leave the lawyer's office."

There was no mistaking the disapproval in his dark eyes now.

"I thought you were going to take a look at the house with me."

She lifted her wrist and concentrated on her watch. "I changed my mind. After thinking about it, I really can't see that I'd be much help. After all, I'm sure the Corbetts must have bought many things since I left, I wouldn't know what was missing. In any case, I'm needed back in Philadelphia."

She looked up in time to see his eyebrows rise. "Philadelphia? I thought you were in Phoenix."

"I was." She started toward the door, putting an end to the conversation. This wasn't the time for explanations. It was doubtful there would ever be a time when she could tell him the truth about Brandon.

Outside in the parking lot the sun warmed her shoulders as she made her way to her car. Even so, she detected a faint chill in the wind blowing in from the mountains. Before long the fall would bring the winter rains and then the snow. How could she have forgotten the clean, fresh smell of the open land and the feeling of losing oneself in the wide expanse of blue sky? It was such a far cry from the burning Philadelphia sidewalks and suffocating buildings that shut out the sunshine.

As she climbed into her car she noticed the dark gray minivan that had followed her out the night before, sitting just a few spaces away. She stared hard at it, wondering what it was about it that had unnerved her the night before.

The Nevada license plate was faded and dented and there were gouges on the door on the passenger's side. Apparently the owner was a lousy driver.

Looking at the van in daylight, however, her fears of last night seemed ludicrous. She had to get control of her nerves, before she did something really stupid.

The roar of Cully's engine made her jump and she started her car. He was already out on the road, heading toward town before she had backed up enough to swing the car out of its space. For a moment she thought he wasn't going to wait for her but he slowed enough for her to catch up before he turned the first corner.

Somehow she got the idea he was mad about something. Well, let him be. She hadn't made any promises. For two cents she'd turn around and head for the airport. After all, there was no law that said she *had* to go to the reading of the will.

Even as the thought occurred to her she glanced in her rearview mirror, tempted to slam on the brakes and turn around. Her hands froze on the wheel. The minivan was right behind her.

It seemed as if all her breath had suddenly deserted her body. Beads of sweat formed on her forehead and the feeling of suffocation was almost unbearable. She clawed for the air conditioner and turned on the fans full blast.

Whoever was driving the van had to have been sitting there while she had been staring at it just a few moments ago. Why hadn't she noticed a driver in the front seat? Had he been hiding, waiting for her to move before pulling out to follow her?

A screech of brakes to her right jerked her gaze from the mirror. To her horror she realized she'd driven right through a stop sign. Cully must have noticed. The driver who'd been forced to brake gestured at her as she went by him, a little too close for comfort.

Thoroughly shaken, she thought about pulling over until she could calm her nerves. Cully's Jeep, however, turned another corner a block away and she had no choice but to follow him, or she'd lose sight of him. Nervously she glanced in her mirror again.

The minivan was gone.

She blinked, staring in disbelief at the empty road behind her. Had she imagined it? No, it must have turned the corner back there, at the stop sign. She followed Cully into the side street and slammed on her brakes as he pulled to a stop in front of her.

Heart pounding, she waited for him, expecting him to climb out and walk back to her car. He was going to give her a ticket. She'd sailed through a stop sign right in front of his eyes.

To her surprise, he jumped down from the Jeep and sauntered over to a faded brick building she remembered was once a warehouse for distributing cut boards from the lumber mills. It had apparently been turned into offices, with new glass doors built into what had once been a solid brick wall.

Cully paused in front of one of the doors and looked back at her, obviously waiting for her to follow.

She pulled in her breath and let it drift out again

before shutting off her engine. Either he hadn't noticed her mistake, or he planned to ignore it. She hoped it was the former. Just to make sure, she scanned the street both ways as she climbed out of the car. There was no sign of the minivan. Surely, *surely,* she hadn't imagined it? Her hands felt clammy as she went through the door that Cully held open for her.

The lawyer's office was a little too cool for comfort and she wished she'd brought a jacket with her. The room smelled of lemon polish and new furniture. An eager young receptionist sat behind a highly polished desk, which was bare of anything except a telephone, a computer and a flashy sign that announced her name was Tanya.

She greeted Cully with an ease that implied she knew him well. Her disapproving glance at Ginny when Cully introduced her suggested Tanya would like to know the town's magnetic sheriff a whole lot better and didn't welcome competition.

She needn't worry, Ginny thought wryly. It was odd that Cully had never married. Mabel had told her he lived alone on his ranch, with just a housekeeper and a couple of ranch hands to help out. She wondered if he had a girlfriend.

She was still wondering about that when Tanya ushered them into a quiet room with somber dark paneling that Ginny found oppressive. The seconds ticked by as she sat with Cully in awkward silence. More than ever now she wished she'd obeyed that impulse to turn her car around and head for the airport.

Would the minivan have followed her out there?

The unbidden thought disturbed her and she

clamped her hands together in her lap. This was a very small town but common sense told her there had to be more than one gray minivan being driven around.

"Don't look so worried. Paul's just going to read the will. As soon as he's through you'll be free to go."

At the sound of his deep voice she'd jumped. She tried to dismiss her ridiculous fears with a careless shrug. "I'm not worried. Just impatient."

"Yeah, I can tell you can't wait to get out of here. I should've remembered how much you hate this town."

For some ridiculous reason she felt like crying. "I don't hate it. I just have things to take care of back home, that's all."

He nodded, his mouth a thin, straight line. "Right."

She was saved from saying anything else when the door opened and a thin, gray-haired man wearing a dark blue suit scurried into the room, murmuring apologies.

Again Cully introduced her and she shook the lawyer's proffered hand, surprised by the strength of his grip. Sharp blue eyes regarded her from behind gold-rimmed spectacles as she sat down again.

"Ms. Matthews, I understand you were married several years ago. Am I right in assuming that Matthews isn't your married name?"

She hesitated, wondering how much she needed to reveal in order to listen to a will being read.

"Ginny's husband died recently," Cully said smoothly. "She's using her maiden name for now."

The lawyer's eyebrows lifted a fraction as he glanced at Cully. "I see. Well, in that case..." He sat down and opened up his briefcase.

Ginny sent Cully a grateful glance, which he barely acknowledged with the briefest of nods.

"Now," Paul Bellman said, smoothing out the sheaf of papers in front of him, "the situation is this. Jim and Mabel Corbett left everything they owned to each other, with provisions in the event of the survivor's death." He began to read the terms of the will, in a dry, unemotional voice.

Ginny tried to follow the legal wording, understanding only the pertinent facts. Jim and Mabel had left certain items to several people, of whom Ginny recognized only three, all of whom had been living with the Corbetts during the years she was there.

The lawyer read out the list of items, some of which Ginny remembered. The pair of silver-plated candlesticks that always stood on a shelf above the fireplace. A white china cat that had lost an ear when one of the kids had thrown a football across the living room. The ancient cuckoo clock that never kept proper time and had to be wound every single day.

Cully sat taking down notes. Now Ginny realized why he was there. If any of those items were missing, it might give him a lead in the investigation. Then again, who would want them? As far as she knew, nothing in that house was worth stealing. Certainly not worth the death of two people. It just didn't make sense.

Then again, if Cully had a list of the items, he really didn't need her there at the house. She could leave with a clear conscience. So why did she have a deep feeling of guilt nagging at her? Why couldn't she forget the eerie sensation of hearing Jim's voice and his urgent message? Why did she feel that there was something she needed to do before turning her back on Gold Peak and everything it had once meant to her?

"And now," the lawyer droned on, "we come to the final provision in the will."

Ginny made her hands relax in her lap. It was almost over. Then, as Cully said, she was free to leave.

"To Ginny Matthews, I leave the house and any contents that have not been disposed of elsewhere, in the hopes that she will find the peace and contentment she deserves."

CULLY STOOD OUTSIDE the lawyer's office, watching two squirrels chase each other in and out of the branches of a leafy maple that had escaped the developer's bulldozer when the warehouse had been renovated.

Ginny was still inside with Paul. She had papers to sign and, he imagined, a dozen questions to ask and he didn't need to be there. Truth was, he felt he needed a good gulp of fresh air.

He'd been just as surprised as she'd looked when Paul had given her the news. He could imagine her shock. It wasn't every day someone was handed a house, free and clear. His very first thought had zapped him like the sting of a whip. Now she'd have to stay awhile longer. She couldn't just take off and leave a house sitting there.

It had taken him no more than a minute or two to amend that. She'd probably hire someone to sell it.

Then again, there was stuff to dispose of. The place was chock-full of furniture. Not to mention shelves and cupboards full of knickknacks. Then there was the stuff Mabel and Jim had wanted to go to some of their former foster kids.

He didn't know how he felt about having Ginny around for a while. She'd made it pretty obvious she was anxious to leave. Seeing her around would only make it harder on him. Too many memories that were best left buried. He'd spent an awful long time learning how to forget.

Deep in thought, he didn't hear her come out of the office until she spoke behind him. "I guess this changes things," she said, in a flat tone that didn't give him any clue as to how she was feeling.

He took his time before twisting his head to look at her. "Congratulations," he said gruffly. "I reckon the Corbetts must have really cared about you."

To his dismay he saw tears glistening on her lashes. An almost uncontrollable urge to take her in his arms made him sound more abrupt than he intended. "I suppose you're going to put the house up for sale."

"I don't know what I'm going to do." She looked down the street and the lost, helpless look on her face squeezed his heart.

"You need some time." He took hold of her arm and led her to his Jeep. "We'll go take a look at the house and you can decide later what you want to do with it."

To his relief she didn't give him any argument. She seemed dazed, as if she were walking in a fog, without knowing what she was doing or where she was going.

He settled her in the passenger seat and then climbed into the cab next to her. "We can pick up your car later," he said as he fired the engine.

She gave him a vague nod then leaned back in the seat and closed her eyes.

He checked his side mirror, waiting for a dirty-looking minivan to roll slowly past him. When it was clear he shifted into gear and glanced at Ginny to check if she had a seat belt on.

His stomach took a nosedive when he saw her expression. She was staring straight ahead, eyes wide, mouth open as if she were uttering a silent scream. He followed her gaze but the road was empty, except for the minivan, which was turning the corner at the end of the street.

"What? What is it? Are you sick?" He leaned over and grabbed her arm and let it go when she flinched so violently he thought he'd hurt her. Now he was really worried. "Ginny? For God's sake tell me. *What's the matter?*"

She was tempted to tell him about the van. If only she could be sure it wasn't just her mind playing tricks, the way it did in her nightmares.

She shook her head. "Nothing. I'm just in shock, that's all. It just blows my mind that Jim and Mabel wanted to leave the house to me."

He had to be satisfied with that answer, although he knew it was a lot more than that. He'd seen fear on her face. Real, intense fear. Something was going on with her and he wasn't going to rest until he found out what it was.

Chapter Four

The Corbetts' house lay half a mile back from the road, hidden by a heavy thicket of pine, alder, cottonwood and dense undergrowth. The hot, dry summer had dried out the uneven trail and the tires of Cully's Jeep bounced over the crusty ruts in the baked earth when they approached the sprawling yard that surrounded the house.

Ginny's jaw ached with tension as they came to a halt in front of the gate. She had been a different person the last time she'd stood at that fence. Eager to begin her new life, determined to put the past behind her, she'd had such momentous expectations. The entire world had beckoned to her with a promise too exciting to comprehend.

Anything and everything had seemed possible. She was going to show Cully and everyone else in that little backwoods town that she, Ginny Matthews, would be someone to look up to and admire. She was finally going to escape the stigma that had poisoned her entire life.

Only it hadn't happened the way she'd planned.

She'd made mistakes. Big mistakes. And she'd paid dearly for them.

"I hope Paul gave you the house keys," Cully said, breaking into her thoughts. "I never thought to ask back there."

She scrambled in her purse for the unfamiliar key ring that held a half dozen keys. "This still feels like a weird dream. I'm looking at the house but I can't believe it actually belongs to me."

"It's in pretty good shape. Jim took good care of it." He opened the driver-side door and hopped down.

Following more slowly, her throat ached with the effort to control her emotions. It didn't seem right to walk up the path to the weather-beaten door knowing that Mabel wasn't there to open it. It was too quiet, too empty without the laughter and shrieks of a half dozen kids swarming around.

The key turned easily in the lock. She had to stop and take a deep breath before she could push the door open. The silence inside the house unnerved her. She couldn't remember a time when the house had been this quiet.

Memories washed over her as she walked into the spacious family room. The silver candlesticks still stood on the shelf above the fireplace, which had been readied for the cold fall evenings to come with a neat stack of paper, kindling and logs.

Tears pricked her eyes. Jim would no longer sit in that creaking old rocker, with the paper on his knees and his glasses sliding down his nose as he peered at the television set in the corner. Never again would Mabel sit in the comfortable armchair opposite him, busily clicking away with her knitting needles.

How many winter nights had they all knelt in front of the fire, fighting for a space to roast fat, squishy marshmallows on the end of a stick? Too many to count.

Behind her, Cully cleared his throat. "Look, if you want some privacy—"

"No!" She couldn't be alone in this house. Not yet. "Let's check out the list of items mentioned in the will. The candlesticks are still here. They're only silver-plated, but a bum wouldn't know that." She turned to face him. "Wouldn't he have taken something like that?"

Cully pulled the list he'd made from his shirt pocket. "That's why I wanted you here to check things out. As far as I can tell nothing's missing. At least, not the usual stuff thieves haul away. The TV set's still here, the stereo and Jim's video camera. The kind of stuff that's easy to sell."

"What other reason could someone have to kill two harmless, elderly people?"

Cully shrugged. "There are a lot of reasons people kill. Revenge, power, money, to cover up another crime, or just the thrill of killing. Someone high on booze or drugs, someone with a vicious temper, who knows? Like I said, without a motive we're more or less dead in the water. But we have to start somewhere. So let's take a tour of the house and maybe you can see something I missed. Something that's out of place, or just looks wrong."

She shook her head. "Cully, it's been at least ten years since I was last here."

"I know how long it's been."

His dark gaze locked with hers and it seemed as if

her heartbeat filled the room. The look in his eyes reminded her of that night long ago, when she'd gone to his apartment to ask him to leave town with her and explore the big wide world out there together.

He'd pulled her into his arms the moment he'd opened the door, his eyes dark with a hunger that had consumed her, as well. They'd fallen onto the bed, their passion wiping away everything in her mind. Until later. Half-asleep, she'd told him of her plans, expecting him to be as thrilled as she was with the idea.

It wasn't as if she hadn't mentioned it before. She'd talked of little else in the days leading up to that night. She'd taken his silence for his usual reluctance to act impulsively. Cully always took his time making decisions, thinking things out, weighing the consequences.

Never for one moment had she doubted his willingness to go with her. It had been the biggest shock of her life when he'd told her his life was in Gold Peak and if hers wasn't, she'd have to move to the city without him.

"Let's get going then." Cully moved away, breaking the spell.

"The cuckoo clock is still there," Ginny said unsteadily.

"Yeah, I noticed." Cully moved around the room, checking his list. "Did Mabel have any jewelry that she might have hidden somewhere?"

Ginny frowned, trying to remember. "Only dimestore stuff. She kept it in a box in her bedroom. I don't think they ever had the money for expensive jewelry."

"Guess we'd better check the bedrooms, then."

She didn't want to be in a bedroom with him. Right now she really didn't want to be in the house with him. "Look," she said quickly, "I know you must have other things to take care of in town. Why don't you give me the list and if I find anything missing I'll let you know."

He stared at her for far too long, making her uncomfortable. "Will you be checking back into the motel?"

"I don't know." She looked around, as if seeking an answer there. Someone must have cleaned up. There was nothing out of place. No smashed lamp, no overturned chairs. She shivered, in spite of the musty warmth in the room. "I might stay here until I decide what to do. I have to call Philadelphia and explain what happened."

"The power's been cut off, and the telephone."

"I have my cell phone." She frowned. "No, I don't. It's in my car. With the rest of my stuff."

"I'll take you back to it, then you can drive back here."

She nodded. "Right. I'll have to buy some clothes if I'm going to stay for a couple of days, anyway. Maybe I will check back into the motel. But I'll come back here first to check out the rest of the list."

To her relief, he gave her no argument. The truth was, she needed to be alone in the house for a while. There were too many ghosts that needed to be laid to rest, too many questions in her mind to be answered.

"I guess the only thing I can do is sell the house," she said, as the Jeep jolted over the ruts on the way to the road. "I'll need a real estate agent to do that for me. Do you know of anyone?"

"There's a couple of good ones in town." He was silent for a moment, then added slowly, "I think Mabel and Jim hoped you'd stay. I figure that's why they left you the house. So you'd have some security. Though I guess your husband must have taken good care of that. Mabel said he was a civil engineer. Made a pretty good living, I reckon."

Her heart skipped a beat. "Yes," she said shortly. "He was and he did."

"Sorry. None of my business. I was just trying to make sense of everything, that's all."

"Well, you're right. It's none of your business."

"Yes, ma'am."

He didn't speak to her again all the way into town.

The mountain road wound down in sharp curves and bends as it dipped into town. She wanted to ask Cully where Jim's truck had gone off the road but one glance at his forbidding expression, the hard set of his mouth and the frown half-hidden by the wide brim of his hat was enough to make her hold her tongue.

It seemed as if they were destined to be at odds with each other. Not that it mattered. She wouldn't be around long enough for it to escalate into out and out war. She'd talk to an agent, make arrangements to sell the house, gather up the items that the Corbetts had bequeathed in their will and drop them off at the lawyer's office, then she could go back to Philadelphia and forget she was ever in Gold Peak, Oregon.

Her rented car still sat outside the lawyer's office and Cully pulled up behind it and killed the engine of his Jeep. The sudden silence seemed unusually dense.

"Thank you," she said stiffly. "I'll let you know if I find anything that might be useful."

"I'd appreciate that." He tipped his hat back with his thumb. "If you want a good agent, try Neil Baumann on Madison. Next to the old movie house."

Once more memory knifed through her. The back row, in the dark. Cully's arm about her shoulders, his warm lips nuzzling her neck. "Oh," she said faintly. "It's still there?"

"The building is, but it's not a movie house anymore. Someone bought it and turned it into an antique store. Pretty fancy one, too."

She wrinkled her brow. "Neil Baumann? Didn't he used to live with the Corbetts?"

Cully gave her a look through half-closed lids. "Yep. I reckon half the town used to live with the Corbetts at one time or other. Neil'd know the house as good as anyone. He's been in the business awhile now. Seems to know what he's doing."

"Thanks. I'll talk to him." She opened the passenger door and swung her feet out to jump down.

"What are you doing for dinner tonight?"

The question took her by surprise. "I don't know... I haven't thought about it... I mean..."

"I'd thought you might want to come out and see the ranch. Lyla, my housekeeper, she's a real good cook. She'd love to show off for somebody other than me and the dogs."

She looked at him, intrigued in spite of herself. "You have dogs?"

"Two of them. A black lab, goes by the name of

Rags, and a mutt we picked up off the highway a while back.''

She had to smile. ''Rags?''

He nodded. ''When he was a pup he'd swing on the drapes by his teeth. Tore them to shreds before I broke him of the habit.''

''I see.'' She was still smiling. ''And what about the other one? What do you call him?''

''Puddles.'' His face remained perfectly straight.

Her laugh bubbled out, surprising even her. ''I hope you've broken him of that habit.''

''Lyla took real good care of that.''

''I bet she did.'' Ginny dropped to the pavement then, on some wild impulse, poked her head back in the door. ''I think I'd like to meet your housemates. They sound like an interesting pair.''

His mouth tilted in a smile and her treacherous pulse leaped in response. ''I'll pick you up at the motel. Five-thirty sound good? It'll give us time for the grand tour before we eat.''

She felt a little breathless when she answered. ''I'll be ready.''

He tipped his hat forward again, gave her a brief salute then backed up with a roar of his engine, made a U-turn and headed back up the street.

Ginny stood for a moment, watching him disappear in a haze of dust. That was stupid. She should have told him she had other plans. But the thought of a nice meal in a cozy house complete with a house-keeper and dogs had seemed infinitely preferable to a hamburger in a cold, lonely motel room. The temptation had been too great to resist.

Right now, however, she had things to do. She'd

worry later about spending the evening with a totally engaging cowboy who had a disconcerting habit of making her forget all the reasons why she shouldn't be enjoying his company.

By early afternoon she had accomplished everything she needed to do. She'd booked into the Sagebrush Motel again, put her return flight on hold and notified Whitman's that she was taking some emergency time off to settle her affairs.

Neil Baumann, the real estate agent, remembered her, although they had spent only a short time together at the Corbetts' house. She remembered him vaguely as being a skinny kid and a pest, always tormenting the girls and occasionally disrupting the meals by violently arguing with anyone who dared disagree with him.

He'd put on weight and had prematurely lost some hair but he was courteous and charming as he assured her he would have no trouble selling the house. "Such a dreadful thing to happen," he said, as he escorted her from his office to her car. "There couldn't be two nicer people than Mabel and Jim. I just can't figure out why anyone would want to hurt them."

"I know. It's all very difficult to understand." She fished in her purse for her car keys.

"Well, if anyone can find out what happened, it'll be the sheriff. He's a good guy and sharp as a tack. He'll find who did this, you can bet your life on that."

She smiled. "I think you're right."

"I don't suppose he's told you if he's got any ideas about who did it? I heard you had dinner with him last night at the Red Steer."

She had forgotten how easily talk got around in a small town and wondered how long it would take for the gossips to find out she was having dinner at the ranch tonight. "I really wouldn't know," she said, as she unlocked the car door. "I'm sure if he did know something he wouldn't be telling me about it. Cops don't usually talk about a case they are working on."

Neil's light blue eyes regarded her curiously. "I heard you got married to some rich dude in Phoenix."

"That's right." She opened the car door, eager to escape the inevitable questions. "Thank you, Neil. I'll wait to hear from you."

"So how come you're living in Philadelphia now?"

"I like the weather better." At the risk of seeming rude, she pulled the door closed and fitted the key in the ignition. As the engine sprang to life, she raised her hand in farewell, barely waiting for him to acknowledge the gesture before pulling away from the curb.

Her mind on the question of where to eat lunch, she slowed to turn the next corner, which would take her into Main Street. Normally her glance would automatically flick to the rearview mirror. Her reluctance to do so now warned her that she still didn't have her jumpy nerves under control.

It had to be all the upset of learning about the Corbetts' deaths and then finding out they'd been murdered. She needed some quiet time, to get her thoughts together.

Changing her mind about eating in a restaurant, she stopped off at the strip mall and bought underwear, chinos, three tops and a cream cotton sweater with a low scoop neck to wear out to the ranch that evening. She refused to admit that for a fleeting moment she'd envisioned Cully's reaction when he saw her in the sweater.

On the way out of town she stopped at a convenience store and bought a ham and cheese sandwich and a six-pack of diet soda. Then she hit the mountain road that would take her back up to the Corbetts' house.

As she swung around a bend in the road she thought she saw a vehicle behind her on a lower slope. It was too far away to recognize but it looked awfully like a minivan.

Determined not to let her dumb fears overrule her common sense, she kept her gaze squarely on the road ahead until she swung off onto the bumpy trail to the house.

She waited until she was almost there before stealing a look in her rearview mirror. The forest stared back at her, thick, green and silent. She was alone.

As she approached the front yard, she took another careful scrutiny of the area before killing the engine. The house seemed so lonely and dejected. A home should have people in it, laughter and love. There was something so sad about an empty house. Even the windows appeared dull and lifeless, like the eyes of an abandoned puppy.

A wave of depression swept over her and she gave herself a mental shake. The past was over and she couldn't bring it back. Once the house was sold a new family would move in and fill the house with happy voices.

She gathered up her sandwich and soda. Her pulse

skittered uneasily when she opened the door of her car. Branches above her shifted in the strong breeze, spraying dead pine needles over the hard ground. Somewhere deep in the woods a blue jay screeched. The rasping sound jarred her nerves. The skin on her arms prickled with apprehension.

Trying to dismiss her irrational fear, she approached the gate and reached for the latch. The hinges squeaked as she pushed it open. She was about to pass through when another sound echoed from the woods behind her. The unmistakable crunch of snapping twigs.

Someone was walking through the trees.

She jerked her head around and scanned the area as far as she could see. No minivan. Nothing but her own car standing just a few feet away. Was it her mind playing tricks again? No. Those footsteps were real. As if to confirm her thoughts, a pair of crows soared from a nearby tree into the sky with a frantic fluttering of their wings.

Galvanized by their hasty retreat, Ginny plunged for her car. She'd locked it automatically before she'd climbed out. Her fingers seemed reluctant to obey her as she fumbled with the keys.

The footsteps drew closer and she scrambled to fit the key in the lock. She could hear them clearly now, just beyond the fringe of trees that would bring the intruder out into the open. With a sob of relief she felt the key enter the lock and turn in it. Just then harsh words rang out behind her and her fingers froze on the door handle.

''Who's there? Whadda you want?''

Although it had been a good many years since

she'd heard the caustic voice, Ginny recognized it instantly. Still shaking, she dropped her hand and turned to face the newcomer.

The withered old man approached her, a shotgun tucked securely under his arm. His beard had grown even longer than she remembered and his tangled white hair reached his shoulders. Old Man Wetherby, the kids had called him. He was a recluse, living alone in an old shack in the woods. She was surprised to see him still alive. He'd always looked as if he were on his last legs.

"Mr. Wetherby," she said, uncomfortably aware of her heart beating way too fast. "It's Ginny. Ginny Matthews. How are you?"

The old man drew closer, his watery blue eyes peering at her in distrust. "You don't look like no Ginny Matthews," he muttered.

"But I am." She tried a wavering smile. "Remember I lived here with the other kids? You used to chase us all out of the woods when I was small. Remember the rabbit I found? It had a broken leg, and you took it home with you."

He drew even closer and Ginny held her breath. She'd forgotten the awful smell that always clung to him. "Well," he said at last, just when she thought she'd have to back away from him, "I reckon you could be Ginny at that."

He nodded at the house. "Corbetts ain't home. They're dead and gone."

His flat statement chilled her. "Yes, I know. The Corbetts left me the house. It's mine now."

He sniffed. "Well, good riddance to 'em. Got what

they deserved if you ask me. That bastard Jim killed my dog.''

Ginny stared at him in disbelief. "Oh, I'm sorry. Are you sure it was Jim?''

"'Course I'm sure.'' The old man lifted his shotgun and shook it at the house. "They killed my Butch. But that ol' dog had the last laugh. His spirit came back and sent them off the mountain. He paid them back.'' His chuckle was pure evil. "Good ol' Butch.'' He peered at Ginny again. "You'd better watch out for Butch's spirit. He's still in that house, looking for Jim. I seen him.''

Ginny swallowed. "Well, I'll be sure to remember that.''

"Yeah, you do that.'' With one last scowl at the house, he shuffled away, mumbling something under his breath that Ginny couldn't catch.

She let out her breath. He'd startled her but at least she knew he was harmless. As a kid she'd been terrified of him but now she felt kind of sorry for him. His long years of loneliness had affected his mind. He was seeing ghosts now. It was sad.

Even so, her heart thumped uncomfortably when she fitted the key in the lock of the front door. Carrying her sandwich and soda into the silent house, she walked into the kitchen, where the counters and stovetop looked strangely bare.

She was used to seeing packages of cereal, rice or spaghetti standing there. There had always been dishes, cups, glasses, piles of newspapers, junk mail and odds and ends scattered everywhere. Whoever had cleaned up had done a good job. Unless Mabel had left it like this, pristine clean, now that she'd no longer catered to a bunch of unruly kids.

Once more her heart ached at the tragic and senseless loss of two good-hearted people, who'd sacrificed so much to help lost kids find their way in an unfriendly world. It wasn't fair. It just wasn't fair.

She slumped down on a kitchen chair and unwrapped her sandwich. It was quiet in the house. Too quiet. She got up and moved to the counter, where a radio sat plugged into the wall. The switch failed to produce a sound and she remembered Cully saying the power had been turned off.

She hunted in the drawers for batteries but couldn't find any. Mabel must have found a new place to keep them. Giving up, she went back to the table to eat her sandwich. She had just snapped the tab on a can of soda when a slight popping sound caught her attention. As if someone had popped the cork on a bottle of wine.

She listened, her head on one side, her heart beginning to pound. Then she heard another and somewhere deep in the house, something cracked.

She made herself relax. It was simply the expanding of aging wood. Heaven knew she'd heard the sounds of it enough times when she was a kid. She could still remember lying in the dark listening to the pops and snaps, her imagination taking her on wild rides of fantasy. One time she'd be on a pirate ship, its sails creaking in the wind. Another time she'd be on a spaceship landing on some distant planet, or beneath the sea in a strange waterworld filled with weird and wonderful creatures of the deep.

Smiling at her childhood fantasies, she reached for

her sandwich, just as another sound froze her hand. A soft thump, as if someone had dropped something on the floor.

For a moment she held her breath, her heart racing. When she heard no more, she made herself relax. Maybe this wasn't such a good idea. She was alone in a big house, at least a mile from the nearest neighbor. No wonder she was feeling jumpy.

She ate half the sandwich, then wrapped up the other half to take with her. After a couple gulps of soda, she started gathering up the items that were to go to the rest of Mabel's beneficiaries.

She'd purchased a large canvas holdall, since she had no room in her garment bag for the extra clothes she'd bought. There was plenty of room in it to hold the candlesticks, the cuckoo clock and the china cat. The next thing on the list was a stuffed bear.

Ginny smiled. She remembered the bear. More than three feet tall, it sat in the middle of Mabel's bed during the day. No one was allowed to touch it, except on special occasions when one of the kids needed an extra dose of comforting. Then Mabel would let the unhappy child lay on the bed, hugging a bear that at times was bigger than the small body holding it. One of those kids must have loved that bear an awful lot to inherit it.

Still smiling to herself, Ginny headed for the stairs, the list in her hand. While she was there, she told herself, she'd look for Mabel's jewelry box, though she had doubts if she'd know what was missing, if anything.

She was halfway up the stairs when she heard the noise again. Another thump, only this time the noise had been accompanied by a scraping sound. As if someone was moving something heavy around.

Chills, as cold as ice, clamped her fingers to the handrail. The sound had come from directly below her. From the basement.

She waited, hardly daring to breath, ears straining for yet another sound to convince her she hadn't imagined it. Nothing. Only the thumping of her heart, so violently her body shook.

She had to get out of here. Out in the sunlight and the fresh air. The rest of the things could wait. She was too upset right now.

Forcing herself to move, she started back down the stairs. She'd reached the hallway when a sharp crack sounded right below her feet.

Something, or someone, was in the basement.

An animal. Yes, that was it. Old Man Wetherby's words came back to her. *He's still in that house, looking for Jim. I seen him.* No, she didn't believe in ghosts. It had to be a squirrel or something.

But squirrels couldn't move heavy objects around.

Staring down the hallway, she peered at the door to the basement. Mabel had always kept the door locked, afraid one of the kids might fall down the narrow, rickety steps in the dark. The only light in the basement was from a bare bulb, with a dangling string to pull the switch on and off.

The door locked from both sides and Mabel kept the key on the ledge above the doorframe—too high for prying fingers to reach—afraid one of the kids would lock themselves in down there.

Ginny looked at the ledge. There was only one way to find out if anything was down in the cellar. One way to convince herself that whatever it was she feared was only in her imagination. Maybe if she faced her fears instead of running from them, she could overcome the nightmares and the gnawing worry that she was losing her mind.

With grim determination, she marched toward the basement door. Balancing on her toes she had to stretch as far as she could to reach the ledge. At first she felt nothing but the smooth wood of the door frame but then her pulse leaped when her fingers closed around the key.

Carefully she fitted the key in the lock. The door swung open with a loud creak that made her jump. She waited, listening, but now everything was quiet and still. *Was someone waiting down there for her?*

Every instinct in her body screamed at her to leave. To run as fast and as far as she could, until she was safely back home in Philadelphia.

Something deep inside her wouldn't let her give in to the inner voices. She had to fight this thing. She couldn't let Brandon win. If she gave in now to the crazy thoughts in her head, he would have the last laugh. She wasn't about to give him that. He had hurt her enough when he was alive. He wasn't going to reach out from the grave to torment her again. Not ever again.

Her hands clenched at her sides, she began to descend the stairs. The shaded hallway behind her allowed little light to filter into the basement. The damp, musty smell wrinkled her nose. She could see nothing but darkness ahead of her. The small window at the back was around a corner and any light that filtered through couldn't reach the steps.

She blinked, trying to adjust her gaze. Shadows seemed to move in the murky darkness. The stairs creaked with each step she took. Her nerves tightened on the very edge of endurance.

She had forgotten how many steps there were. She couldn't see where they ended. Her hand outstretched in front of her, she stepped down one more. Then a sudden sound made her blood run cold. A soft scraping sound in the darkness.

Her heart pounded, throbbing in her ears. Pain pounded her forehead. She froze, unable to go down or back up. She had been crazy to come down here without a flashlight. Too late she remembered the power had been cut off. Even if she'd found the string to light the bulb, it wouldn't have gone on.

She started to back up the stairs. Then, from somewhere in the dark shadows of the room behind her, she heard a sound that iced her bones. A whispering voice, terrifying in its warning. *You can't escape me. You are going to die.*

Chapter Five

Ginny's shuddering cry of fright bounced off the walls and followed her as she bolted up the stairs. Racing headlong down the hallway, she had only one thought in her mind. Escape. Away from that house and its whispering memories.

She flung herself out the door and down the path, fumbling with the latch on the gate for several anxious seconds until she had it open. She left it unlatched, her one driving purpose to reach her car and get out of there.

Her fingers shook so badly she dropped the keys and had to scramble in the dirt for them. At last she had the door open and she fell into the seat, almost slamming the door on her feet in her haste to shut it.

As she gunned the engine she shot a nervous glance at the front door of the Corbetts' house. She'd slammed it shut behind her. It was still firmly closed. No one had followed her out. She was safe.

Even so, as her car jolted forward, she took a frantic look around, half-expecting to see the gray minivan parked somewhere near the house. Nothing. No van. No car. No sign of anyone in the area except herself.

In spite of her efforts to calm her racing pulse, she drove too fast down the mountain road, rocketing around the bends at a pace that normally would have alarmed her. Every minute or two she glanced in the rearview mirror, certain she would see the minivan pursuing her.

As she turned onto the main road, a school bus loomed ahead of her. The sight of something so normal finally slowed her heartbeat. She eased the brake down until she was cruising at a reasonable speed behind the bus.

This was crazy. She had to quit doing this. The noises could have been anything. The wind, which she now noticed tossed the branches of the ponderosa pines along the edges of the highway. It could have caused a tree limb to scrape against a window. A squirrel leaping to the floor could have made a thump loud enough for her to hear.

Now that she had time to really think about it, she could see how stupid she was being. How could someone be in the cellar if the door had been locked and the key still on the ledge?

It must have been that squirrel, or even more likely, a rat. And the voice? She shuddered. It must have been her imagination after all. Which brought her back to the thing that terrified her the most. Mentally unbalanced, they called it. A nice way of saying she was slowly going insane.

CULLY HAD SPENT the afternoon going through all the records of former foster children who had been as-

signed to the Corbetts. It was almost five o'clock
when he finally closed the files. Leaning his elbows
on his desk, he ran his hands through his hair. Some
of those kids were still living in Gold Peak.

Luke Sorensen, who worked at Bailey's Garage
and helped out at the Red Steer. Sally Irwin, who also
worked at the Red Steer. Neil Baumann, who sold
real estate. And a half dozen more. The rest were
scattered all over the country. Two had died. Three
more were living in a foreign country.

He'd been hoping to find something, no matter how
small, that might possibly be a connection to the murders. So far he'd come up empty. None of the files
had given him a clue as to who might have killed Jim
and Mabel. Because of the lack of forced entry he
was assuming the Corbetts knew their attacker. But
he couldn't eliminate the possibility that they let a
stranger into their house. It all came down to one
thing. Motive. If he knew that, he'd at least know
where to start looking.

He shoved his chair back and picked up the pile of
folders. Enough for today. He had a dinner guest to
worry about now. Though he couldn't figure out why
in the world he'd invited Ginny Matthews to dinner
at the ranch.

It had seemed like a good idea at the time. He
needed to know what it was she was taking such pains
to hide. He was thinking that she might just relax
enough to tell him in the comfortable environment of
his living room.

He had to be out of his mind. Asking for trouble,
that's what it was. Even Lyla had sounded surprised
when he'd called her to warn her about their unex-

pected guest. And she didn't even know about their past. Then again, how long had it been since he'd invited anyone out to the Black Diamond? He couldn't remember.

He glanced at the oak-framed clock on the wall. It would have been nice to go home and take a shower before picking up Ginny. Change into something a bit more classy than the jeans and checkered shirt he'd worn all day. But the ranch was a good half hour's drive away and it was almost time to head for the Sagebrush.

At the thought, he felt a twinge of anticipation. In spite of his reservations about the coming evening, he was looking forward to it with an eagerness he hadn't felt in a long time. Maybe he was heading into trouble but there was no reason he couldn't enjoy the ride while it lasted. Impatient with his juvenile thoughts, he crammed his hat on his head and headed out the door.

Ginny was waiting in the foyer when he walked in the door five minutes later. She stood in front of a rack of travel brochures, studying one of them with a frown of concentration that he remembered well. She had a habit of massaging the back of her neck when she was tense. Right now her hand worked on her neck as if she were trying to rub the skin clear off.

He paused for a moment, drinking in the sight of her. She wore pale khaki pants belted low on her hips. Her sweater stretched tight across her breasts, the neckline dipping just low enough to make his mouth water.

He'd never expected to see her again. Now he was looking at her just a few feet away from him and he'd never wanted her as badly as he did right now. He took a deep breath and let it out on a sigh.

She must have sensed him standing there as she turned her face, her cheeks flushed. Her gaze locked with his and he wondered if she knew what she was doing to him. Or if she cared.

The thought brought him back to reality with a crash. He took two steps toward her then paused as she moved toward him. "Ready to go?"

She nodded, her glance sliding away from him as if she were afraid to look at him. "How far is the ranch?"

He followed her out to his Jeep, trying not to notice how her hips swayed as she walked. "About half an hour. Lyla's looking forward to meeting you. She's got great plans for supper, so I hope you're hungry."

"I am. I only had half a sandwich for lunch."

Something about the way she said it caught his attention. He gave her a sharp look. The years he'd spent enforcing the law had honed his instincts to such a pitch that the slightest tremor in a voice alerted him. Something had upset her since this morning. Something significant.

He held the door open for her while she eased her hips into his Jeep. Deep in thought, he climbed in next to her and gunned the engine. She'd planned to go back to the house that afternoon. He wondered if she'd seen something that might have a bearing on the murder. If so, he hoped like hell she'd volunteer the information and he wouldn't have to pry it out of her.

"What's the name of your ranch?" she asked, as

they headed out of town and onto the dry, dusty rangeland that spread away from the mountains.

"The Black Diamond." He pressed his foot to the accelerator to coax more speed out of the reluctant vehicle. "It was just the Diamond Ranch when I bought it. I added the Black. Made it sound more personal."

"I like it." She stared out of the window as if she'd never seen the flat meadows of the high plateau before. "What kind of ranch is it?"

"Horses. It's not a big ranch. Just enough to keep me and a couple of hands busy when they don't need a sheriff in town."

"Does that happen very often?"

"More often than not. Jed and Cory, my deputies, can usually handle anything that crops up. We don't get too many murders in McKewen County. Not enough people for them to go around killing each other, I reckon. We leave that to the city folk."

The minute the words were out of his mouth, he wished them back. He'd made up his mind he wouldn't keep harping on about the past tonight. There was far too much in the present he wanted to talk about. And the past had too much bitterness tied up in it for them to have anything to say about it.

He waited for Ginny to come back with a sharp retort but to his surprise she said quietly, "Then you're extremely lucky."

"Yep, I reckon we are at that." He glanced sideways at her. The window on her side was down a few inches and the wind's greedy fingers ruffled her hair. He liked it better that way than the smooth, flawless style she'd worn that morning. A woman's hair should look natural, flowing soft and free. The kind a man loves to run his hands through.

He forced his mind off the image of her lying next to him on the bed, her hair spread over the pillow while he combed it back from her face with his fingers. "Looks like the wind's getting up," he said, in an effort to get his mind back to a less dangerous subject. "Could be a change in the weather."

"You think it's going to rain?" She looked up at the empty sky as if expecting a downpour any minute.

"Not yet. We're only halfway through September. We haven't been getting any rain until late October these past few years." He frowned into the rearview mirror, his gaze on the mountains behind him. "Last winter we had hardly any rain at all. And it's been a long, dry summer. Everything is tinder dry. If we start getting some of that dry lightning that's been lighting up the mountains lately, we could be in for some real trouble."

"Like a wildfire?"

"Yep. You must remember the one we had when you were living at the Corbetts'. For a while there we thought we'd lose the house."

She nodded. "I remember. All that smoke got into the house and it smelled terrible for weeks afterward. The worst part was watching all the animals running away from it. I cried myself to sleep thinking about the ones who didn't get away."

"Yeah, I know." His mind flicked backward in time to a hot summer night after the main danger of the fire had passed. Ginny had been just a kid then, too young for him to have the kind of feelings he'd dealt with later. But that night he'd heard her crying and he'd crept into the room she'd shared with Sally to comfort her.

Sally was asleep but Ginny had looked at him with such agony on her face he'd felt like crying, too. She'd finally fallen asleep with his arm around her and he'd had to shake it like crazy to get the feeling back in it. He'd never spoken about it afterward to anyone. And neither had she. When he'd mentioned it to Sally years later, she had no memory of it at all. He glanced at Ginny, wondering if she was remembering that night, too.

She was staring into the side mirror, craning her neck to get a better look.

He peered into the rearview mirror to see what she was looking at but the road was empty behind him. Yet still she stared at the mirror, as if she were waiting for something to appear, something that she didn't want to see.

"Someone following us?" he asked lightly.

He'd meant it as a joke but she jumped as if she'd been stung by an angry bee. "What? Of course not! I mean…" Her voice trailed off into what sounded awfully like a groan.

Concerned now, he gave her a hard look. "Isn't it time you told me what's eating you?"

She leaned back in her seat, the closed look he'd dreaded hiding her expression. Her voice sounded normal again when she spoke, though he noticed her hands were clenched in her lap. "I don't know what you mean. Nothing's bothering me."

"I know all this business with Mabel and Jim is upsetting you. If there's anything I can do to help…"

"It's not that."

For a moment he thought she was going to tell him what was on her mind but when he glanced at her again her lips were clamped tight as if she'd let the words slip out and had instantly regretted it.

He took a wild shot in the dark. "You must be missing your husband a lot."

He was watching the road and didn't see her expression change but he heard the terse note in her voice when she answered him. "You'd think."

"But you're not."

It was a statement more than a question and she didn't deny it. "Brandon and I had...problems. It wasn't a good marriage."

"I'm sorry." There were a hundred things he wanted to say but he kept quiet, hoping that his silence would encourage her to say more. He was disappointed when she leaned forward in her seat, asking, "Is that your ranch over there?"

He shook his head. "That's my neighbor, Jim O'Connor. I'm another mile or two down the highway, and then five miles after the turn."

"What made you buy a ranch?"

He shrugged. "I had to do something with my spare time. I've always loved horses, as you well know." He shot a glance at her. "Do you still ride?"

She shook her head. "I haven't been on a horse since I left. There's not much opportunity for riding horses in the city."

"Yeah, I know. It was the thing I missed most when I lived there."

He could hear the wariness in her voice when she answered. "You've never talked about living in the city. Except to say how bad it was."

He'd never told her about his younger days. He'd never talked about it to anyone after he'd been sent to the Corbetts' house. When Ginny had asked him about his life before he came to Gold Peak, all he'd told her was that he'd run away from home as a kid and had ended up with the Corbetts. Just like her.

"I lived for a while in Portland, when I was real young," he said, wondering why he was telling her now.

"Were you born there?"

"Nope." He wished now he hadn't mentioned it but since he had, it seemed only right he should tell her all of it. "I was seven years old when my father was transferred to Portland. Until then we'd lived in Prairie Falls."

"Is that in Oregon?"

"Yep. It's smaller than Gold Peak. At least, it was when I lived there. My best friend's family had a horse ranch, and I spent all my time there."

"You must have missed that."

"I did. I was pretty miserable, I guess."

He sensed her looking at him, but he kept his gaze on the road ahead. The turn was coming up any minute.

"I can understand why you were unhappy, but not everyone hates the city the way you do."

He hesitated, then said slowly, "Well, that's not all of it. A couple of years after we moved there, my father left us to go live with a woman he'd met at work."

"Oh, I'm…sorry."

She'd sounded shocked. Her genuine sympathy encouraged him to finish the story.

"I guess everything fell apart after that. My brother got into trouble and was sent to a remand home."

"I didn't know you had a brother."

Now she sounded a little hurt. He flicked a glance at her.

"I didn't like talking about that part of my life. I had better things to talk about back then."

She snatched her gaze away from him. "Where is he now?"

Cully shrugged. "Who knows? We lost touch. I tried to find him when I was elected sheriff, but had no luck. He could be dead for all I know."

"What about your mother?"

He let out his breath on a long sigh. "Well, after my dad left, she got a little wild. Started drinking and partying half the night. She brought her boyfriends home with her and she didn't want me around to spoil her fun. One morning she got mad at me over something and told me she wished I'd never been born. Said I was an embarrassment to her and I was stopping her from living her life. That night I packed a bag and tried to hitch a ride back to Prairie Falls. I haven't seen her since."

"Oh, Cully." His pulse leapt at the distress in her voice. "That's terrible. You must have been heartbroken."

He shrugged. "Not really. I was glad to be out of there."

"I remember you telling me you ran away from home, and got picked up by a cop."

"Yeah. Frank Manelli. Great guy. He knew the Corbetts and got me into their home. He even put in a word for Rich, my brother. Got him into a work program on a farm somewhere. I knew right then that I wanted to be a cop. If it hadn't been for Frank, I would have ended up like Rich, on the wrong side of the law. I guess I wanted to make that kind of difference in people's lives, too.''

She didn't answer him but just sat there staring through the windshield with a wistful look on her face that made him long to know what she was thinking.

''Well, here it is,'' he announced, as they approached the gates leading up to the ranch. ''Welcome to the Black Diamond. Get ready for a rowdy welcome from the dogs. They're not used to female company.''

She stole a look at him. ''No girlfriends?''

''Not in a while, anyway. Haven't had much time lately for socializing. The ranch keeps me pretty busy.'' He pulled up in front of the three-story house and shut off the engine. The front door opened almost immediately and a chorus of yelping and barking accompanied the two dogs that rushed down the porch steps and bounded over to the Jeep.

Cully jumped out and closed the door. ''Okay, you two, calm down and show the lady some manners.''

Ginny had scrambled out the other side and was under attack from Puddles, who seemed intent in leaping right up to her face. Rags had all four paws on the ground but was trying to push his nose into her hand.

She laughed at them and crouched down to their level, which was pretty gutsy of her, considering the way they were all over her. She didn't seem to mind that Rags was licking her face, or that Puddles had his paws all over that pretty sweater.

He liked that, Cully decided, as a warm glow crept into his heart. This was more like the Ginny he remembered. The carefree country girl who didn't mind getting messy as long as she was having fun.

She looked up at him at that moment, laughing and trying to say something while Rags slopped kisses all over her face. He felt as if the sun had changed direction and was coming up all over again, lighting up everything it touched.

"If he's not going to introduce me, I'll have to do it myself." The short wiry woman standing at the bottom of the steps wagged a finger at him. "Shame on you Sheriff Black. You're forgetting your manners."

Ginny straightened at once and held out her hand. "You must be Mrs. Whittaker. Cully told me you are an excellent cook."

"Did he now." The housekeeper's light brown eyes flicked over at him. "Trust a man to think of his stomach first." She shook Ginny's hand. "Call me Lyla. Let's go inside. I have some cheese puffs and a nice bottle of wine waiting for you. That should hold you both until dinner is served."

Cully followed the two women up the steps, grinning at his housekeeper when she sent him a meaningful look registering her approval of Ginny. He felt good. Better than he had in a very long time.

He would have to be on his guard tonight. Being alone with Ginny could play tricks with his mind. No matter how badly he wanted her, for his own peace of mind he had to keep his distance. He wasn't about to be caught in that trap again. In a few days she'd be back to her city life and he'd be just a faint memory. He'd do well to remember that tonight.

GINNY PAUSED in the doorway of the vast living room and looked around in wonder. She wasn't sure what she'd been expecting—stark furniture, heavy paneling, gun cabinet, deer heads and stuffed fish on the wall—the sort of thing one expects from a man living alone.

Never once had she imagined the thick green carpeting, the pale gold couches, or the magnificent landscape above a glistening white marble fireplace.

"This is beautiful," she murmured, as she moved closer to examine the painting. "What a lovely room."

"Glad you like it." Cully stood in the doorway and it was hard to imagine him relaxing in this room with its soft hues and silky drapes. "I don't use it very often. I spend most of my time in the den."

"Which is just as well," Lyla said from behind him. "Can you imagine the dogs all over those couches?" She pushed past Cully and carried the large tray she was holding over to a long, rectangle coffee table. "Here, Ginny. Sit yourself down and have a glass of wine while you wait for the sheriff to get presentable."

Cully pulled a face. "Never could get her to call me by my name." He glanced at his watch. "Give me five minutes, Ginny. And don't eat all the cheese puffs before I get back."

He disappeared and Lyla shook her head. "It's been so long since he did any entertaining, he's forgotten how." She poured a generous amount from the bottle of Pinot Gris into a glass and handed it to Ginny. "Now you just sit there and relax. I have to go feed the dogs, or they'll be bouncing around in my kitchen looking for food." She set the wine down next to the two bottles of beer that she'd apparently brought for Cully, then hurried out of the room.

Left to herself, Ginny took a sip of her wine. This house was such a contrast to the scruffy apartment where Cully used to live. The transformation took her breath away. It wasn't just the furnishings, though they certainly added charm to the room. It was the feeling of tranquility, a sense of security that she hadn't felt since she'd left the Corbetts' house all those years ago.

It must mean so much to Cully. Her heart had ached for him earlier, when he'd told her about his childhood. She'd had no idea he'd been through so much. No wonder he hated the city. He probably blamed city life for everything that had gone wrong.

She was so happy that he'd found contentment here in Gold Peak. Though he must be lonely at times. Not that it seemed to bother him. Some men preferred to live alone. Though she never would have thought Cully was one of them.

The wine tasted good and she took another sip. This was nice. This was very nice. She reached for a cheese puff and popped it in her mouth. Cully was right. Lyla knew what she was doing.

She was on her second cheese puff when Cully returned, freshly shaven and wearing a black shirt with his jeans. At the sight of him, her pulse quickened. He'd slicked his dark hair back but already strands of it fell across his forehead. He looked more relaxed, more approachable, more like the Cully she remembered.

He leaned over the table to refill her glass and she caught a breath of his cologne. The earthy fragrance embodied his rugged nature—forceful, proud and just a little primitive.

Everything about him was so vital, so masculine. She could envision him on horseback, thundering across the rangelands with his head bent against the wind, his hat sheltering his face, his strong thighs guiding the eager animal beneath him.

She shivered inside, remembering the touch of his hands on her body, confident yet tender, stirring a fire that had never quite died.

He looked up at that moment, surprising her. Something sparked between them, an invisible thread of smoldering energy that seemed to bond them together, like a soldering iron melding lead.

His body stilled and she saw the fire reflected in his eyes, in his soul. She knew he'd felt it, too, and seemed to be waiting for her to make the next move. *No, not again.*

She felt her cheeks burn and sat back on the couch, her glass clutched in her hand. Casting about for something to say, anything that would break the awkward silence, she said quickly, "I'd like to see Sally again. Does she work full-time at the Red Steer?"

A mask seemed to fall over his face and he picked up a bottle of beer. Carrying it with him, he sat down on the couch opposite her. His voice sounded husky when he answered her. "She works most days there. Goes in for the lunch hour, then leaves until around five, and stays until they close. She'll be happy to see you."

Ginny nodded. "She must be upset, too, about the Corbetts' death."

"I reckon she is. Most of the townsfolk were at the funeral. Jim and Mabel were pretty well known in Gold Peak."

"Well, they'd lived here most of their lives." She sighed. "I still can't believe they're gone. They're the only real family I've known."

"What happened to your family? You never talked about them when you were growing up."

For a moment she hesitated. He'd told her about his past. She owed him that much. "It isn't a pretty story," she said at last. "My mother was unmarried and very young when she had me and her parents didn't want to take care of me, so I ended up in foster homes. I'd been through a lot of them before I got to the Corbetts. They were the only ones who really made me feel they cared about me, even though I had to share them with so many others."

"I know what you mean." His smile chased away the bad memories, making her feel warm inside. "The Corbetts had that knack for making every kid feel special. I just wish I could get my hands on the bastard who killed them. I'll never rest easy until I have him under lock and key."

"You found no clues at all when you searched the house? Fingerprints? What about DNA? Isn't that supposed to be the big new technology for catching crooks?"

"It is, but you have to have something to match it up with. There were fingerprints all over the house but none of them matched up with any known criminals. The crime lab from Rapid City went over the place pretty thoroughly. They're still working on the evidence, but they don't have a whole lot to go on.''

He paused and set the bottle down on the table. ''I don't suppose you saw anything today that might help?''

At his words, she was reminded of the terror she'd felt standing on the steps to the basement. The last thing she wanted to do was talk about it. On the other hand, she'd promised herself she would confront her fears and the best way to do that was to bring them out in the open. Maybe if she talked about it, she would see how irrational she was being.

Maybe if she told Cully about it, she wouldn't have this irrational fear that she was slowly and inevitably losing her mind. She only hoped he would understand. She couldn't bear it if she saw the disbelief in his face that would prove her fears were justified.

Chapter Six

"When I went back to the house this afternoon," Ginny said slowly, "I was going to collect all the items that the Corbetts had willed to other people and take them to Paul Bellman's office."

She paused remembering her fright at the sound of footsteps in the forest. "Just as I got out of the car Old Man Wetherby came out of the woods. He scared me half to death."

Cully wrinkled his brow. "I'm not surprised. That old buzzard spooks a lot of people. What the heck was he doing at the Corbetts' house?"

"I don't know. I didn't think to ask him." Quickly she recounted her conversation with the old man.

Cully was frowning when she finished. "Sounds as if he was on a vengeance kick."

"I can't believe Jim killed his dog." She leaned forward to put her glass down on the table. "Jim loved animals."

"Jim didn't kill anything. Wetherby's dog got into Jim's chickens. Killed three of them before Jim got him out of there. He called me. The law says if a dog kills, it has to be put down. Once they kill they're likely to do it again. We had no choice.''

Ginny felt a tug of sympathy for the old man. ''He must miss him,'' she said soberly.

''I guess he does. I think I'd better have a word with him, though. No one thought to question him about the murders. He might be a little weird in the head, but he's always been harmless enough.''

Ginny caught her breath. ''You don't think he shot the Corbetts, do you? I know he had a shotgun, but then he's always carried one. That's why we were all so scared of him when we were kids.''

''I'm not ruling anything out right now.'' He reached for his beer again. ''When a man's mind has gone, there's no telling what he's capable of.''

Her stomach turned at his words. She had to force the next words out, striving to keep a light note. ''Speaking of going out of your mind, I thought I heard strange noises coming from the basement this afternoon.''

Cully's expression changed at once. A sharp gleam appeared in his narrowed eyes. ''What kind of noises?''

Talking about it brought back the fear after all. She reached for her glass, swallowed a mouthful of wine and set it down with a hand that shook. ''I don't know. Small thumps, a scraping sound, as if someone was moving a heavy box or something.''

''Did you take a look?''

''I started to.'' She swallowed, striving to steady her racing pulse. ''I know it's silly, but I've been imagining all sorts of things lately. There's a minivan parked at the motel and I keep seeing it on the road, as if it's following me. Last night when I went to the graveyard, I could have sworn someone was chasing me. And then, the noises in the basement. I think my mind is going.'' She tried to laugh but only succeeded in sounding hysterical. Quickly she picked up her glass and took another gulp of wine.

''Whoa, take it easy.'' Cully leaned forward, his elbows on his knees, his face creased in concern. ''I'm not surprised you're imagining things. You've been through a lot lately. What with losing your husband, and now Jim and Mabel being murdered, it's no surprise that you're jumpy.''

She nodded, fighting the ridiculous tears that were on the verge of spilling over. ''I keep telling myself it's all in my mind, and that I'm being stupid.''

''Come on, Ginny, you're not stupid. This is a small town. You see the same car buzzing around and in your state of mind it's easy to imagine it's following you.''

She made a small sound of distress. ''My state of mind?''

''Aw, crap. I didn't mean it like that. You know I didn't. I only meant that anyone who's been through what you have is likely to imagine all kinds of weird things.''

''But they seem so real.''

''Well, you could have heard real noises. There's probably a rat or something down in that basement.''

Eagerly she grasped the vindication. ''That's what I thought. And the scraping sound could have been a branch against the window. After all, there's trees all around the house and the wind was getting up.''

''You got spooked because you were there alone,

that's all. Rattling around by yourself in a big old house like that would make anyone feel creepy. Did you finish up there or do you have to go back?''

"I have to go back. I haven't finished collecting up the legacies in Mabel's will, and there are a couple of things I'd like to take back with me to Philadelphia.''

A shadow seemed to cross his face. "Right. Well, I'll go back with you next time. I don't like the idea of you being there alone. And first thing in the morning we'll get the power put back on. Neil's going to need it anyway when he shows the house.''

"Thanks.'' She managed a grateful smile. "I could have used you this afternoon. I had to stand on my toes to reach the key to the basement, and even then I had to stretch to get it.''

He gave her a puzzled look. "What happened to the key in the door?''

Now it was her turn to look baffled. "There wasn't one. Mabel always kept the key on the ledge above the door. That's where I found it.''

"Then she must have had more than one key. When I searched the house, there was one already in the lock of the basement door. I used it to open it, and left it in there.''

A pulse began throbbing in her temple. "Maybe someone from the crime lab took it out.''

He shook his head. "I was the last one to leave. I locked up the house behind me. Nobody had access to that house until Paul gave the keys to you.''

The throbbing spread all over her head. "Then what happened to the basement key?''

Cully looked grim. "That's what I'd like to know.

I'd better take another look at that cellar. I could be jumping to conclusions, but I'm pretty sure a rat wouldn't use a key to get in there.''

Her heart had started its tattoo on her ribs again. ''But if you locked the house, how would anyone get in?''

''Good question.'' He drummed his fingers on the table. ''Guess I'll have to check out the house more thoroughly. There could be a window unlocked somewhere. Or broken. Then again, I guess, if it was the killer come back, he could have taken a house key with him when he left.''

Ginny shuddered. ''I'll have the locks changed on all the doors, just in case.''

''Good idea. And first thing in the morning I'll go over the house again. There's not much point in going tonight. I wouldn't see much without power in the house.''

Feeling somewhat reassured, Ginny did her best to relax. Cully was right. There wasn't much they could do about it until the morning. Until then, she would just have to try and keep it all out of her mind.

AFTER TAKING Ginny on a tour of the house and the stables to see his beloved horses, Cully escorted her to the dining room, where they enjoyed the tasty meal Lyla had served up for them.

The shrimp salad was followed by roast pork and apple sauce and now Cully sat across the table from Ginny, sharing a pot of steaming, fragrant coffee.

Both dogs lay on the rug near his feet, Rags snoring with his head on his paws, while Puddles lay on his side, twitching every now and again in his dream-filled sleep.

It was a warm, peaceful feeling to sit there and watch Ginny's changing expressions in the glow of candlelight—another of Lyla's special touches. He could get used to this, Cully thought. He could get used to seeing her at his table, in his living room, riding his land, lying in his bed. Especially lying in his bed.

There'd been a moment earlier, when he'd been so tempted to touch her face, to lean in and kiss that inviting mouth, to take the fleeting moment and stretch it into whatever she was willing to share.

In that moment the memories had pounded his mind—hot, searing memories that tormented his body and stirred his hunger. What they'd had back then had been so damn good. The need to find out if it was still like that between them was like an instrument of torture and just as unbearable.

Aware that he was slipping into a treacherous frame of mind, he clamped down on the tantalizing thoughts. He'd been down that road before. He'd learned a hard lesson and he couldn't afford to forget it. The pain of saying goodbye wasn't worth a few days of passion, even if she were willing to go along with it. He knew full well that she would never be happy trapped in a small town like Gold Peak and he would be miserable living in the city. Either way, in time, after the first excitement of being together had faded, they'd be at each other's throats. Just like the last time.

He'd seen what that could do to people—what it

had done to him—and it just wasn't worth the heart-ache. Not again. Never again.

He made an effort to focus on what she was saying. She was talking about her job and it all sounded too complicated for him to follow.

"It's very difficult to judge what clothes women are going to buy ahead of time." Ginny said, reaching for the coffeepot. "By the time they're picking out their fall clothes we're already ordering for spring. We have to be constantly one step ahead of them, and with fashions and preferences changing all the time, it makes the decisions pretty tough to call."

"Mostly guesswork, then."

She smiled. "Pretty much."

For a moment he was held by the way her lips parted to show a row of even white teeth. With a struggle he forced his mind back to more mundane matters. "So, how did you meet your husband?"

The smile vanished at once. At first he thought she wasn't going to answer then she said quietly, "I was a receptionist in his company. We met at a company picnic when we were paired in a scavenger hunt."

He hadn't meant to ask. The question had been on his mind ever since she'd walked into the Red Steer but he hadn't meant to ask. He forced interest into his voice. "Did you win?"

Now he could see pain in her eyes. Her voice was barely above a whisper when she answered. "No. We got…distracted. We didn't even finish."

He felt as if one of his horses had kicked him in the gut. He didn't want to know any more, yet he couldn't seem to quit asking the questions. "So how did he die? What happened to him?"

She played with her coffee cup for several long seconds then a shudder shook her body. It was no more than a slight tremor but he noticed it.

"He was piloting his private plane," she said, just when he was about to break the tense silence. "No one knows quite what happened. Engine failure, electrical problems, whatever it was, it was too sudden for him to make contact with anyone. He went down in the mountains, somewhere in Idaho, I think. The plane crashed and burned. The search parties didn't find him until two weeks later. By then he was unrecognizable."

Shaken, Cully let out his breath. "I'm sorry. It must have been a heck of a shock for you. So that's why you moved to the east coast, to get away from the memories?"

"Not exactly." The flame from the candle flickered, sending shadows chasing across her face. She sat back, as if to escape the revealing glow. "I might as well tell you. I left Brandon six months before he died."

"Oh." He didn't know what to say next. Conflicting thoughts chased through his mind. Regret that she'd been that miserable, and grim satisfaction that another man hadn't made her happy after all. "I'm sorry."

She shook her head. "It was the right thing to do. We…weren't happy and…" Her voice trailed off and again his instincts nudged him. She wasn't telling him all of it. Part of his mind warned him that it was none of his business and if he probed, she'd probably tell him that. He was reluctant to lose the cozy, intimate atmosphere that he was enjoying, maybe a little too much. On the other hand, curiosity had always been one of his less desirable traits and he burned to know what had gone wrong with the marriage.

Carefully, he poured himself another cup of coffee. "It must have been pretty bad for you to take off on your own and go clear across country. Why didn't you come back to Gold Peak? At least for a while. I'm sure Mabel would have loved to take care of you."

Again that odd silence before she answered. When she did, her words seemed to drop like ice chips, chilling the warmth of the room. "I didn't come back here because I was afraid my husband would find me."

Now it all made sense. That look in her eyes he'd noticed last night. The reluctance to talk about what had happened to her since she'd left. The way she'd avoided talking about the man she'd married. "He beat you," he said, unable to keep the fury out of his voice.

"If I didn't do everything he said…yes. He beat me."

She'd spoken so calmly, with such indifference, she could have been talking about the weather. His fists curled on the table. "Then the bastard deserved to die."

She didn't answer and he struggled to contain his anger. "Why did you marry him? Didn't you have any idea—"

"No!" Her voice rang out across the table, startling him. "Do you think I'd have married him if I'd known? Of course I didn't. When we first met he was so charming, so kind, so considerate." She paused, as if she were struggling for the words to explain. "You have to understand. All my life people had treated me like a leper. My own family wanted nothing to do with me. Every foster home I was sent to found fault with me. They said I didn't fit in, I was hard to handle...any excuse to be rid of me. Until I went to the Corbetts, anyway."

"That doesn't mean you're a bad person—"

"Maybe not. But I was sure treated like one."

And he had let her down, too. She hadn't said it but the words were there, hovering between them like angry bees waiting to attack. He tried to think of something to say, anything to take that look off her face but before he could find the words she went on talking, in that low, fierce voice that echoed her bitterness.

"I wanted people to look up to me. I wanted to be someone people admired and respected. Brandon had money, respect from everyone who knew him. He was an important man, and he was in love with me. At least, he told me he was. For the first time I felt important, too. It wasn't until after I married him that I realized what a terrible price I was paying for all that prestige."

Again the anger gripped him. "What happened?"

She shrugged. "He was possessive, jealous, controlling. Everything had to be done his way and in his time. I had to have his permission to do anything or go anywhere. I had to account for every single second of my time, and if he wasn't satisfied with my answers he beat the right ones out of me. When I threatened to leave him, he swore he'd kill me first before anyone else had a chance with me. So I left in the middle of the night, got as far as I could go and I changed my name. My whole identity.''

Cully's throat was too tight to form words. Seconds ticked by while the only sound in the room was Rags's quiet snoring.

Then Ginny added softly, ''When I got the news of his death, it was as if I'd been let out of prison. For the first time in more than ten years, I was free. I didn't have to be afraid anymore.''

Finally Cully found his voice. ''You never had kids?''

''No.'' The pain was etched on her face now and his heart ached for her. ''Thank God. Brandon didn't want anything to take my attention away from him.''

''How did you find out he'd died?''

''Jim told me. I didn't tell them where I was, but I called them often from my cell phone. Jim said that an investigator with the FAA called him. He told Jim that Brandon was dead. Apparently he had filed a flight plan before he left. He was alone in the plane, on his way to discuss plans for a new bridge in Idaho. Had I still been with him, I would have died, too. He never went anywhere without taking me along. The investigator told Jim that all that was left of Brandon's belongings were his wedding ring and the watch I'd given him for an anniversary gift. My name was on the back of it. He thought I would want them.''

Cully didn't want to think about that. ''So then you called the investigator?''

''No.'' She took a sip of her coffee and put down the cup. ''I never did. I didn't want anything that belonged to Brandon. Not his watch, not his ring, not his money, not the house, nothing. Ginny Pierce was dead. I was Justine Madison. The death of Brandon Pierce had nothing to do with me.''

''Well, I'd say you were well rid of him.'' It wasn't what he wanted to say but it was the safest right then.

''Yes, I suppose I am. If only I could get rid of the nightmares as easily. They still haunt me. Day and night.''

''Maybe you should talk to someone. You know, someone who knows how to help with that kind of thing.''

''You mean a shrink?''

Her face looked so stricken he hurried to reassure her. ''No, not a shrink. A doctor, perhaps. He might be able to give you something to help—'' A low growl from Rags interrupted him.

He glanced down at the big dog. ''What's the matter, boy?''

Rags lifted his head and growled again. At his side, Puddles rolled over and stood, his short brown ears pricked and his feathery tail alert.

Cully frowned. Something had disturbed the dogs. Maybe a coyote howling in the distance, though he hadn't heard anything. He glanced at Ginny. She was watching the dogs with the same odd look she'd worn that morning in his Jeep.

What was it she'd said earlier?

There's a minivan parked at the motel and I have the feeling it's following me.

Maybe she hadn't imagined it after all. She certainly hadn't imagined the missing key. Now that he thought about it, he seemed to remember a minivan passing him outside the lawyer's office.

Rags growled again and got to his feet, his fur rising in a furry ridge between his shoulder blades. Cully rose with him. "Stay here," he said briefly. "I'm going to take a look around."

She nodded, her fingers white as they clasped her cup. She looked scared and yet there was a defiant tilt to her head that dared anyone to mess with her. It was a gesture he'd seen a lot in the past. It heartened him to know she hadn't lost that gritty streak of courage.

No one was ever going to hurt her again. Not if he could help it. He wasn't sure exactly how he was going to achieve that but right then it was enough to make that promise to himself.

He left her alone in the dining room and headed for the back door. Rags was ahead of him already, his growl erupting into a warning bark. Puddles yapped in unison and the second the door was opened, both dogs streaked outside like bullets from a shotgun.

Lyla spoke from behind him. "Whatever's the matter with those two tonight?"

"I don't know," Cully said grimly. "But I aim to find out." He paused long enough to grab a flashlight from the closet by the door, then he was outside, listening to the throaty barking of the dogs. There was no doubt they were excited about something. It could be a coyote disturbing the horses, though he couldn't hear them whinnying—a sure sign that they were uneasy. Switching on the flashlight, he raced after the dogs. Above his head a huge cloud covered half the moon. Even so, there was enough light to see the dogs at the fence, both of them standing with their feet braced apart, hackles raised and barking like crazy. Something was out there and by the sound of it, whatever it was had no business being there.

INSIDE THE HOUSE Ginny listened to the faint barking of the dogs, twisting her cup round and round in her fingers. She'd been on edge ever since Cully had told her about the missing key. If Cully was right, then it was possible she hadn't imagined the noises. There could have been someone in the basement while she was in the house. The thought made her flesh creep.

It could have been the Corbetts' killer. Didn't murderers sometimes return to the scene of the crime? She shuddered at the thought. At least she had the compensation of knowing it wasn't her mind playing tricks.

Then again, if she hadn't imagined the noises in the basement, what about the rest of it? Did that mean the footsteps in the graveyard, the minivan and the voice whispering her name were all real, too?

Confused now, she wasn't sure if she preferred the thought of losing her mind or dealing with a real stalker out there. Either one was a terrifying prospect.

The sound of the dogs scampering back through the kitchen brought a measure of relief. Right then she didn't want to be alone. Lyla's cheerful voice called out from somewhere. "What was it, a coyote?"

Cully's gruff answer was too low to hear but now the dogs were in the dining room, nudging her knees with their noses, eager to be petted. She obliged, leaning down to reach Puddles's silky ears with one hand, while scratching Rags's head with the other.

"Looks like you got yourself some new friends."

She raised her chin to find Cully standing in the doorway watching her with a guarded expression in his eyes that worried her. She dropped her gaze to the dogs again. "Did you see anything out there?"

"Nope." He came back to the table and sat down, reaching for his coffee. "The dogs chased around for a bit, sniffing the ground like something had been there, but it was too dark to see beyond the fence."

He paused and her pulse skipped. "What is it?"

His frown vanished and he smiled at her. "Nothing. I guess I'd better get you back to the motel."

She glanced at her watch, surprised to see it was so late. "I'm sorry, I had no idea." She got up from the table, bringing both dogs to their feet again, tails wagging. "I should have driven myself out here. It will take you over an hour to drive back to town and home again."

"That's okay. I'm used to it." He waited for her to thank Lyla for the delicious meal and receive a wet and slobbery farewell from the dogs, before ushering her out to his Jeep.

"Come again," Lyla called out as Ginny climbed into the car. "This place is far too quiet without company."

Ginny waved to the housekeeper, who waited until Cully had started the engine before closing the door, shutting the dogs inside the house.

"I like your house," Ginny said, as they started down the narrow road that led to the highway. She'd been impressed by the guest rooms on the top floor of the house. The sloping ceilings and dormer windows added an old-world charm to the bedrooms and the old-fashioned bathroom had a footed tub that she adored.

"Thanks. It's kind of big for one person, I guess, but I like having all that space around me."

"Lyla does a good job of taking care of it."

"She's been with me for five years now." Cully changed gears and the Jeep speeded up. "I was lucky to find her. Her husband died right about the time I bought the ranch. Sally told me Lyla was looking for a job housekeeping. I needed someone to take care of the ranch, so it worked out well for both of us."

"I'm surprised you don't have a wife to share that lovely home." It had to be the wine, she thought, loosening her tongue. Normally she would never have uttered that thought aloud.

She hoped that he'd ignore the comment and change the subject. Instead, she heard him say quietly, "I guess I never found anyone interested enough in that position."

There was that awkward silence again. In order to break it she said brusquely, "There are worse things than living on your own."

"So I hear."

He'd sounded angry and his next question told her why. "Why did you stay with him so long? Eleven years is a long time to put up with that kind of brutality."

She thought about it. "I guess I was afraid he'd come after me and carry out his threat. It wasn't until I got really desperate that I found the courage to take the risk."

"There is such a thing as police protection, you

know. He must have left marks, bruises. Didn't anyone ask about them?"

Her throat ached with the effort to keep her voice steady. "I didn't see much of anyone. When I did go out I covered everything up with makeup. I know it's hard for you to understand, but he was a powerful man. I was afraid of what he'd do to me if I told anyone."

"The bastard."

The muttered curse was strangely comforting. "It doesn't matter anymore," she said unsteadily. "He's dead now, and he can't hurt me anymore."

"It's what he's done to your mind," Cully said fiercely. "He's changed you, made you afraid. The Ginny I knew was never afraid of anything. Or anyone."

"You think I'm paranoid, too," she said miserably.

"No, I don't! Of course I don't." His voice was harsh, startling her. "I didn't mean that. I believe the noises you heard in the house today could have been real."

"What about the minivan, and the footsteps in the graveyard?"

She could tell by his momentary silence that he was uncomfortable. "Ginny, right now I can't honestly say what I believe. All I know is that two innocent people were murdered, for no apparent reason. I'll get to the bottom of it. That's a promise. You can trust me on that."

Yes, she thought, with a little rush of warmth, she would gladly trust him with her life. She clung to that thought all the way back to town, while Cully chatted about his ranch and the horses he loved so much.

"You should come out again, take a ride with me and see the rest of the spread," he said, as they pulled into the parking lot of the Sagebrush Motel.

"I'd like that." She'd spoken automatically, her gaze raking the parking lot for sight of the gray minivan. There were only a half dozen cars parked outside the motel, hers included. None of them looked remotely like a minivan.

"What about tomorrow? Right after we check out your basement. You can pick up the stuff for Paul while we're there, and then we could have lunch before we head back to the Black Diamond. Maybe drop in on the Red Steer so you can see Sally."

His words penetrated and she tried to calm the uneasy pounding of her heart. "That sounds wonderful. I'd love that. I haven't been riding in so long, though. I hope I remember how."

"Easy as falling off a bike." His face, reflected in the light from the streetlamps, looked stern, as if he were already regretting the invitation.

Now she felt awkward again. "Thank you, Cully. I enjoyed this evening very much. You were right about Lyla. She's a wonderful cook. And the dogs are so adorable."

"Our pleasure, ma'am. Glad you had a good time."

"Well, good night." She thought about offering her hand but after tonight it seemed too formal. Instead she reached for the door handle. "I guess I'll see you tomorrow morning then?"

"I'll pick you up around nine-thirty. That will give you time to have some breakfast."

"I'll be there."

She opened the door, just as he added, "I'll come in with you, just to make sure everything's okay."

A chill of apprehension chased away the warm glow. She didn't argue but dropped to the ground, her gaze once more probing the shadows in the parking lot.

Now she was glad of his company as they walked over to the shabby building. The wind tossed the branches of the cottonwoods, making them whisper and sing in the quiet of the night. She was on edge— listening for sounds that weren't there. All she could hear was the quiet hum of a car engine passing by on the highway and the echo of Cully's boots on the pavement.

The rows of flimsy wooden doors looked vulnerable, a fragile barrier to the rooms within. She was letting her jumpy nerves get to her again, she told herself, as she led Cully to the door of her room. He waited for her to unlock the door and she had trouble finding the key in the depths of her purse.

The door had a deadbolt lock. Obviously the owner of the Sagebrush wasn't investing in anything as modern as a card slot. With fingers that weren't too steady, she fitted the key into the lock.

To her dismay, it wouldn't turn, no matter how hard she jiggled it. "This place should be pulled down and rebuilt," she muttered, giving the door an angry thump. The door swung open, startling her.

Stepping inside, she slid her hand along the wall and felt for the switch that would turn on the lights. Conscious of Cully right behind her, she stepped into the room, then stopped short, ice shooting through her veins at the sight that met her eyes.

Cully bumped into her, then muttered, "What the—?"

Ginny's lips felt frozen as she tried to answer him. Every drawer in the cheap dresser had been pulled out onto the floor.

The mattress had been thrown from the bed, lying on top of the covers heaped beneath it.

Broken glass littered the floor in front of the television, which had a huge gash in the screen. Her garment bag had been ripped open, her clothes scattered everywhere. It looked as if a pack of wild dogs had rampaged through the room, destroying everything in their path.

Cully pushed past her and strode to the bathroom, cursing when he opened the door. On shaking legs she followed him and peered past his shoulder. Everything she'd left in a neat row—hairspray, cosmetics, comb, brush, toothpaste and toothbrush—all of it lay trampled on the floor.

She made a little sound in the back of her throat.

He whirled around and it seemed so natural when he folded his arms around her, as if they had both been waiting all night for it to happen.

"Well," Cully said softly, "I reckon we can rule out your worries about being paranoid. Whoever did this is a real person, all right, and by the looks of it, he's pretty serious."

Chapter Seven

Cully's deputies arrived a few minutes after he placed the call. He introduced them to Ginny and she shook hands with both of them, aware of their curious glances as they went about the task of dusting the room for fingerprints.

Cory, a tall, lean man with piercing blue eyes and a quick smile, seemed to remember her, though she couldn't place him.

"I remember you in school," he told her, his keen gaze darting about the room. "Feisty little thing you were back then."

Cully cleared his throat. "Let's make this quick, guys. We need to clear up this place so Ms. Matthews can get to bed."

The look Cory sent Cully was totally lecherous.

Cully ignored it but Ginny wasn't about to let them get the wrong idea. "Cully was giving me a ride home," she said, staring Cory in the eye. "If he hadn't been here I would have walked in on this alone."

"Uh-huh." Cory's tone made it obvious he wasn't buying her explanation.

Jed was more polite. "Not a very good welcome to our little town, ma'am." He jammed a thumb under the brim of his hat to lift it above his brow. "Can you tell me what's missing?"

"Nothing, as far as I can see." She gestured at her garment bag and the scattered clothes. "That's pretty much all I brought with me. Anything of value, like my credit cards and cash, I had with me in my purse."

"No camera, jewelry, gifts you might have bought?"

She shook her head. "Whoever did this went to a lot of trouble for nothing."

Jed exchanged a meaningful glance with Cully. "Yeah, well, we don't get too much petty crime in this town. Too bad he had to pick your room." Jed walked over to the open door of the closet and peered inside. "We'll get this taken care of, Cully, and be out of your hair in no time."

Cully looked grateful. "Thanks, Jed. Meanwhile I'd better go talk to the manager." He nodded at Ginny as he walked to the door. "I'll be right back."

She watched him leave, wishing she knew what it was Jed had communicated to him.

Cory seemed absorbed in what he was doing, while Jed attempted to make conversation with her as he worked. Ginny was too shaken up to pay much attention to what he said.

Before long Cully was back, his expression serious. Both deputies looked up as he walked through the door.

"Anything?" Jed asked.

Cully shook his head. "The guy heard nothing, saw

nothing. I'm not surprised, considering how loud the TV was blaring.''

''Well, we'll check these out and get back to you in the morning. By the way, the lock on the door was forced open. That's why the key wouldn't work.'' Jed sent Ginny a smile. ''Good night, ma'am. Hope you can get a good night's sleep after this.''

''Yeah,'' Cory murmured as he followed Jed out the door. ''Sleep well, you two.''

Cully sent him a lethal glance, while Ginny pretended she hadn't heard the sly dig.

The door closed behind them, leaving her alone with Cully. Right then she badly needed a hug. That moment earlier had been all too brief. Just when she was beginning to enjoy the sensation of being in his arms, he'd let her go and become thoroughly businesslike.

Looking at his face now, the intent frown between his dark brows, she wondered if he'd even realized he'd been holding her.

He stared at the floor, apparently deep in thought. Before she could ask him what was on his mind, he said abruptly, ''I guess we can clean up this mess now.''

He started replacing the drawers and she picked up her clothes to throw back into them. Her garment bag was ruined and she dumped it back in the closet, making a mental note to buy a new one.

Cully crouched in front of the TV, gathering up the broken glass. She left him to the task and headed for the bathroom. Her hands shook as she replaced all the items back on the shelf. Although Cully was in the next room, she felt defenseless, her quivering nerves jumping at the slightest sound. She couldn't wait to get out of there, back where she could feel his comforting strength, his calm assurance.

Finally she had everything picked up. Cully had replaced the mattress when she went back into the room and was struggling to spread the covers evenly over the bed.

She hurried to help him, flinching at the sight of pieces of jagged glass in the trash basket. "I'm glad you were with me. I wouldn't want the manager to think I did this. He might have had me locked up for vandalism."

"He would've had to get past me first."

She tugged on the bedspread to straighten it. "Of course. I keep forgetting you're the sheriff."

His face puckered in a wry grimace. "You wouldn't if you were around Lyla enough. She never lets me forget it."

She managed a smile. "Doesn't she ever use your first name?"

"Nope. It's always Sheriff, or if she's talking to someone else, Sheriff Black. Doesn't matter what I say, she won't change it."

"She's probably proud of the fact that she takes care of a sheriff. It's a prestige thing with her."

He gave her an odd look. "Prestige. Sure seems to mean a lot to you."

She felt her cheeks flush. "It used to." She finished straightening the bedspread then looked around the room. "Thanks for cleaning up in here."

"My pleasure." He sat down on the bed then shifted his hips, bringing one knee up on the bed. "We need to talk. There's a few things I need to ask you, then I'll get out of here and let you get some sleep."

She knew, without question, that sleep would be difficult, if not impossible in that room again. She sank down opposite him. "I can't believe this. I've never been robbed before."

"This doesn't look like a regular robbery." He gestured at the broken television set. "Whoever did this was pretty angry about something. A common thief would have taken that TV, not put his foot through it."

His words gave her an uneasy spasm under her ribs. She pulled her feet up on the bed and wrapped her arms around her knees. "I don't understand."

He took off his hat and laid it on the bed, then ran his hand through his hair. The gesture left little spikes standing up. For a moment she was distracted by the urge to reach out her hand to smooth them down.

"I think he was looking for something," Cully said quietly. "Something he didn't find in the Corbetts' house."

Cold fingers of fear touched her spine. "You think it was the same person?"

"It sure looks like it. The way the room's vandalized but nothing seems to have been stolen. If we can find fingerprints here that match some of those in the Corbett house, then we might have a better idea."

Now she was truly frightened. "What was he looking for?"

"I was hoping you'd be able to tell me." His gaze seemed to sear her mind. "Did you take anything out of the Corbett house yesterday?"

"No, nothing. I was going to bring the things Mabel had mentioned in her will, as I told you. When I got spooked by those noises I ran from the house. The bag I put the stuff into is still there.''

"Did Jim or Mabel send you anything recently? A letter, a gift, something that might be unusual?''

"Nothing. They couldn't. They didn't know where I lived.''

"Did Jim say anything about meeting someone new, or having a visitor?''

"No, I don't think so.'' She concentrated, trying to remember the conversations she'd had with Jim over the past few weeks. "The most unusual thing he told me was about the call from Brandon's lawyer. But that was three months ago.''

Cully frowned. "Did your husband ever meet the Corbetts? Did he visit them, or talk to them on the phone?''

"Not until after I left him. We were going to come back and visit them but then…'' She hesitated, reluctant to finish.

"Then what?'' Cully prompted gently.

She stared hard at her hands. "The first time Brandon…hit me, I called Mabel. I was hysterical. Jim wanted me to come home, and he got really angry with me when I wouldn't go. I tried to tell him Brandon would follow me and I was afraid of what he might do to me, but Jim wouldn't listen. He kept saying he'd take a shotgun to him if he ever showed his face. I made them both swear on the bible that they wouldn't tell anyone.''

"And they didn't,'' Cully said, so fiercely she looked up at him.

"I didn't want anyone to know what a terrible mistake I'd made,'' she said, wondering why she was trying to defend herself.

''Right. The prestige thing again.''

That hurt. She pressed her lips together to stop the fiery words of resentment. This wasn't the time for that particular argument.

''So he called them after you left him to find out where you were?''

''Yes, he did. Several times. That's why I didn't tell them I was in Philadelphia, or that I'd changed my name. They couldn't tell him what they didn't know, no matter what he threatened to do. I don't think he ever visited them, though. Jim would have told me if he had.''

An uneasy silence settled in the room. ''I have a hunch there's a connection here somewhere.'' After long seconds ticked by, he lifted his head. ''Who investigated the crash that killed your husband?''

Taken aback by the abrupt question, she had to think for a moment. ''I don't know. The FAA I guess. Why?''

''Was there ever any indication that it might not have been an accident?''

She sat facing him now, her knees under her chin. Eyes wide, she stared at him. ''Are you saying that someone sabotaged Brandon's plane?''

''I don't know what I'm saying, except that I don't believe in coincidences when it comes to murder. First your husband dies, then your foster parents and now someone trashed your room.''

''But the Corbetts had never met Brandon. What possible connection could they have with him?''

He gave her a long, intent look. ''You.''

"Dear God." She buried her face in her hands. Her voice was muffled when she spoke again. "Could I be responsible for the deaths of Mabel and Jim?"

"Ginny, you know full well that whoever killed them is responsible, not you."

"Why doesn't that make me feel better?" She dropped her hands. "But why, Cully? What on earth could I have that someone wants badly enough to kill for it?"

"You might not have anything. Maybe our killer just thinks that you do."

"It just doesn't make sense. Nothing makes sense anymore."

"Look, at this point I'm shooting in the dark. I may be way off track. Maybe I'm wrong and what happened here tonight had nothing to do with the murders. Maybe your husband's crash was an accident, and it's all just a coincidence. In any case, I'd feel a whole lot better if you moved to another room for tonight, this time up on the second floor. Get your things packed and we'll go see the manager again."

It felt good to be doing something and she managed to stuff everything into the garment bag. Although it wouldn't zip up, Cully fastened it with his belt, then offered to carry it to her new room on the second floor. Now she couldn't wait to get out of that room with its shattered television and broken lamp. She still didn't think she could sleep but at least she'd feel better knowing that if the intruder came back, he wouldn't find her in that room.

The manager was obviously annoyed at being disturbed again, though he did his best to hide it. "Never had a break-in until tonight," he told Cully, as he entered the new room number into his computer. "I always thought this was a peaceful, law-abiding little town. Now, what with a double murder and this here break-in tonight, I'm beginning to think it's time to move on."

"I'm sure we'll catch whoever did this," Cully said, as he held the office door open for Ginny. "Then we'll put him in jail so he can't bother anyone again."

The manager looked skeptical. "Yeah? Well, what about the guy who killed those two people on the mountain? When are you gonna find him?"

"We'll find him, too," Cully said harshly. "That I can promise you. And he'll pay for what he did."

The manager nodded, apparently satisfied with that answer.

Ginny's new room was on the second floor at the very end of the building. Conscious of Cully's footsteps ringing out beside her as she trudged the length of the balcony, Ginny wished he would say something, anything, that would make her feel this wasn't just another case he was working on but that he had some personal feelings toward her.

She wasn't sure what she had expected from this evening. On the ride home she'd been conscious of a vague feeling of disappointment, as if the visit to his ranch hadn't lived up to expectations. Yet if someone had asked her, she couldn't have said why.

All she knew was that Cully had changed. He'd grown a tough, hard shell that she couldn't seem to get through. There had been a moment or two when she'd seen flashes of the sweet, affectionate boy she'd once known but the brief instances had vanished before she could acknowledge them. He was doing his best but somehow she knew that the past would always be a point of contention between them, something that might never be resolved.

Maybe if they'd had time, they could have hashed it all out and come to some kind of understanding. But in a few days she would be flying back to Philadelphia, with no reason ever to come back, and the gulf between them would be wider than ever.

She was a fool to ever think it could be otherwise. If he'd had any feelings for her at all, he would never have let her go so easily in the first place. What made her think that it could be different now? She couldn't answer that. All she knew was that she wanted it to be different. That ever since she'd boarded the plane to fly home, she'd hoped that they'd both grown up enough to overcome their differences.

Maybe she'd hoped for more. If so, she was a bigger fool than she'd thought.

"You'd tell me if you knew anything, right?"

His deep voice startled her and she realized they had reached the door to her room. Confused by the question, she frowned at him. "About what?"

"About what this guy might have been looking for." He regarded her with a shrewd expression that made her squirm. "Are you sure you're telling me everything? Ginny, if you know something, anything that might help with this case, you have to tell me."

Inexplicably, her temper flared. "Dammit, Cully, if I knew don't you think I'd tell you? If someone's looking for something, whatever it is, I certainly haven't got it. I don't know what it could be. I don't have anything that belongs to Brandon, or the Corbetts, either."

"It could be something you know. Some kind of information that could be vitally important to someone."

Exasperated, she raised her voice. "Listen to me. I don't know *anything*. I wish to hell I did. I want to know what this is all about every bit as badly as you do. Probably more."

Apparently unmoved by her violent reaction, he shrugged. "Okay. I had to ask."

He waited until she had the door open and the lamps switched on, then carried her bag into the room, where he deposited it on the bed.

"Thank you." She felt awkward, angry at him without really knowing why.

She watched him reach into his pocket and pull out a notebook. "I'll give you my number at home. Call me if you need me."

"I'll code it into my cell phone."

He gave her a disparaging glance. "This isn't the city, Ginny. Cell phones don't have much coverage out here."

She tightened her lips, resisting the urge to lash out at him. He just couldn't let it go. He had to keep digging.

"Sleep well." He moved to the door and looked back at her. "I'll see you in the morning."

She didn't know if she wanted to see him tomorrow. Or ever. It was painful and she'd been through enough pain lately to last her a lifetime. Nevertheless, she needed to see this thing through now. If Cully was right, she had become personally involved in the murders now and she wasn't about to leave until they got to the bottom of it.

"Thank you for the ride home. And for everything you did tonight."

He didn't answer her but touched the brim of his hat with his fingers in a mock salute then strode away from her down the balcony to the steps.

Left alone, she stepped inside the room and closed the door. It was too quiet, too lonely. She switched on the clock radio that sat by the bed and left it on, as well as the lamp beside it while she tried to fall asleep.

She must have drifted off, as she awoke with a start to find the radio buzzing softly. The station must have gone off the air. Yet she could still hear voices somewhere. Someone in the next room must have the television on. She could hear screams, shouts. The shrill bleeps of an alarm.

Heart thumping, she sat up in bed. Light, brighter than the soft lamplight, flickered on the walls. Now she could smell it. Pungent, acrid, stinging her throat. *Smoke.*

She lunged out of bed and dashed to the window. The drapes squeaked in protest as she dragged them back and peered outside. She hadn't imagined it. Thick gray smoke billowed up from the floor below and now she could see flames licking at the steps at the end of the balcony.

Sick with fear she dragged the door open, choking as the smoke wreathed around her. Behind her the smoke alarm shrieked a warning, its strident bleeps ringing in her ears.

Farther down the balcony a door opened and an elderly couple wrapped in robes stepped out. They were coughing and looking around in confusion.

In the distance a siren wailed, while from somewhere in the parking lot a hoarse voice shouted over and over, "Fire! Fire! Get the hell out of there... *now!*"

Shaking so hard she could hardly stand, Ginny raced back inside the room and pulled on her pants and the sweater she'd taken off earlier. Luckily she hadn't unpacked more than her toothbrush. She knew that seconds were vital if she wanted to escape the fire. She grabbed her purse and the garment bag and hauled them out of the room.

The other couple were coming toward her when she emerged on the smoky landing. The woman coughed and wailed pitifully, while her male companion wrapped his arm around her in his attempt to reassure her.

"Can't go down the steps," he told Ginny when they drew close. "They're on fire."

Ginny raised her voice above the woman's wailing. "What about the fire escape?"

He shook his head. "No good. It's at the other end of the building. Can't get to it."

Just then the siren howled louder as a black car slid into the parking lot and came to a screeching halt. The siren mercifully died, while red and blue lights cut through the darkness in a wide swathe.

Ginny recognized Cory and Jed as they leaped from the car. She wondered if they'd notified Cully. It would take him at least half an hour to get out here. She thought about calling him herself but just then a muffled explosion sounded from below and the woman screamed. "We have to get down, Marty.

We're going to die!'' She started running toward the flames.

Marty chased after her and caught up with her. In spite of her flailing arms, somehow he managed to hold on to her.

"Look," Ginny called out, "we'll be alright. Someone's got a ladder." She pointed to the manager, who was dragging the ladder over to the balcony.

The elderly man looked over the railing and shook his head. "It's not big enough," he called out hoarsely. "It won't reach."

Watching him struggle with his terrified companion, Ginny felt a sudden calm, as if she were witnessing the scene from a great distance, completely detached from her body.

She threw her purse and garment bag over the railing and raced up to the couple.

Marty was still fighting to hold on to the woman. The poor woman offered little resistance when Ginny grabbed her arm. The fit of coughing that racked her body with deep, rasping convulsions had taken all the fight out of her. Tears streamed down her face as she struggled to breathe.

"Look, we don't have much choice." Ginny put an arm around the woman to support her. "Your wife is on the point of passing out."

"We're not married," the man said shortly. "But if we get out of this, I'm going to make her my wife." He shook the frail woman, forcing her eyes to open. "You hear that, sweetheart? *Rosie?* We're going to get married."

Rosie stared at him as if he were out of his mind, then promptly fainted.

The ladder clanged against the railing, the top rung below the level of the floor. The side supports trembled precariously with the weight of someone climbing up.

Cory's face appeared over the edge of the floor. "We have to hurry. There's not much time."

Ginny took hold of the fallen woman's arm again. "Help me get her over the railing."

Luckily the unconscious woman's thin frame carried little weight. Cory hauled himself over the railing and together the three of them struggled to balance her on his broad shoulders. "Fire engine's on the way," he said, as he started back down with his heavy load. "Should be here in a few minutes."

By then it would be too late, Ginny thought, sending a nervous glance to the other end of the building which now seemed engulfed in flames. She prayed the rest of the guests had escaped and that no one was trapped in that deadly heat.

Just before Cory's face disappeared beneath the level of the floor he looked up at them. "Can you two make it down by yourselves?"

"We'll manage," Ginny assured him, speaking for both of them.

Marty weakly agreed.

"Just wait until I'm near the bottom. I don't know how this ladder's going to hold up with the weight."

Ginny nodded and Cory disappeared from view.

Leaning over the railing with her elderly companion, Ginny waited until the deputy was two thirds of the way down then turned to Marty. "You next. I'll help you over the railing."

"Women and children first," Marty insisted. "I

won't—'' the rest of his words were lost in a fit of coughing and wheezing. Alarmed, Ginny gave him a little push. "You go. I'll never get you over the railing if you pass out."

He started to argue again but Cory yelled up from the parking lot. "Get down here! That roof's gonna cave in any minute."

With one last desperate look at her, Marty hooked a leg over the railing.

Using all her strength, Ginny pushed and shoved, then held on to his shoulders until his feet were steady on the ladder.

"Don't wait," he said, his voice rasping painfully. "Come down with me."

"I'm right behind you. Just *go!*" The railing felt hot as she clung to it and watched Marty inch his way down, pausing every now and then as the coughing racked his body.

Cory had reached the ground and laid his burden down. He knelt over her, feeling for her pulse. Over by the car Jed talked urgently into his radio. Marty was halfway down now, moving at a snail's pace.

Cory looked up and yelled again. "Ginny! You've gotta come down *now!*"

Just as he spoke, a thundering roar shook the floor beneath Ginny's feet. She turned to see the far end of the building collapsing in flames and then the thick black smoke rolled over her, blinding her, choking her.

Gasping and coughing, she clawed for the railing. Tears streamed from her eyes and she bent double as a fit of coughing threatened to cut off her breath entirely.

Someone below her yelled, "Jump! We'll catch you!"

Balanced on the rail, one foot groping for the ladder, she considered the option. Where were the fire engines? *Where the devil was Cully?*

And then she heard his voice. He was below her somewhere, shouting her name, though she couldn't see anything through the dense smoke. Just the knowledge he was there gave her strength.

She clambered onto the ladder, the deep rasping coughs threatening to shake her grip loose and throw her to the ground. One rung down, then another. She couldn't breathe. She couldn't hold on.

Strong hands gripped her ankles, then her thighs, then her waist. A firm body slammed into hers and his voice was harsh in her ear. "Let go, Ginny. I've got you."

His fingers pried hers from the ladder and then she was hoisted on his shoulders. Shuddering coughs tore at her lungs and she could hear a horrible wheezing noise that she realized was coming from her chest.

She was on the ground and someone was fastening something over her nose and mouth. At last she could breathe. She closed her eyes and let the soft darkness take her away.

Chapter Eight

Her throat and mouth stung, as if she'd been chewing sandpaper. With an effort she opened her eyes but the bright light dazzled her and she quickly closed them again.

Water. Dear God, she needed water. She turned her head and cautiously opened her eyes again. Cully sat on a chair by her bed, his eyes closed, his chest rising and falling in the rhythm of a deep sleep.

She tried to speak but could produce nothing more than a hoarse whisper. Her hand seemed to move of its own accord, reaching for his knee.

As she touched him he started, his eyes flying open, his body already leaning forward before he was properly awake. "Ginny. Thank God."

She heard the relief in his voice and smiled. It was nice to know he'd worried about her. "Where are we?"

"Hospital. Rapid City." With bent elbows he flexed his arms, then reached for a large plastic mug with a straw poking out of it. "The nurse said you could have a couple of sips of water when you woke up."

"Please."

Sliding his arm under her head, he raised her shoulders so she could drink.

The water tasted better than the most expensive bottle of champagne. The cool, wet liquid soothed her throat and gratefully she swallowed a couple of mouthfuls before drawing back from the straw. "Thank you." Her voice was still a rasping whisper and she cleared her throat, wincing at the pain.

"Don't try to talk." Gently he eased her back onto the pillow and withdrew his arm. "The doc said your throat would hurt for a while. She'll give you something to help that."

"How…long…?"

He glanced at his watch. "You've been out for about three hours."

"Am…I…?"

He understood at once. "You're doing fine. Doc says you should be able to leave today if you feel up to it. Apart from some smoke inhalation, you got away pretty lightly. You were damn lucky."

Now he sounded angry. She peered up at him. His scowl confirmed it. "What—?"

"Sshh!" He reached for the water again and once more she was treated to the comforting strength of his arm holding her shoulders.

Already she was feeling better. The water went down more easily this time and although her lungs ached and her stomach muscles hurt from all the coughing, she definitely felt stronger.

"Thank you," she said, gratified to hear a faint semblance of her voice, one stage better than the whisper.

She waited until Cully had sat down again before trying again. "Marty and Rosie?"

Cully frowned. "Who?"

"You know, the elderly—" A cough interrupted the sentence, stinging her throat again.

"I told you not to talk. I'll leave if you don't quit trying."

She nodded, her gaze anxious on his face.

"They're both here, and doing fine. Luckily there were only a handful of people staying at the motel. If it had been the height of summer, there might have been more tourists passing through."

"My purse? Where—?"

His warning frown silenced her. "In the Jeep, along with your clothes, though I'm afraid that overnight bag of yours is headed for the trash."

She relaxed, knowing that at least she still had her credit cards and her airline ticket home.

"More water?"

She shook her head.

"I reckon you won't be going back to the Sagebrush. By the time the fire engines got there, it was pretty well burned down." He yawned, then got to his feet. "Guess I'd better let you rest. It'll be dawn before too long and they start bringing breakfast around early in this place."

She didn't want him to leave. He looked exhausted and she realized he must have been up all night. "Thank you," she whispered again.

His eyes looked bleak when he looked at her. "Why didn't you call me?"

"There wasn't time."

She coughed again and he held up his hand. "Okay, I'm going. Get some sleep."

He turned to pull aside the green curtain that surrounded her narrow bed.

"Wait!" The word came out as a croak but he paused to look back at her. "You saved my life. Thank you."

His smile made her feel better. "Just doing my duty, ma'am." He crammed his hat on his head. "Look, I don't know how long you plan to stay here, but since you have nowhere else to stay for the time being, you're welcome to stay out at the ranch. We have plenty of room and Lyla would enjoy the company. I reckon the dogs would like it real well, too."

She wanted to take him up on the offer. Oh, how she wanted to, if only he'd given her some inclination that he wasn't just being polite. Lyla and the dogs. He hadn't said if *he* wanted her to stay.

Apparently taking her hesitation for indecision he said lightly, "You don't have to make any decisions now. Think on it, and let me know what you want to do."

She nodded and he raised his hand in a brief farewell before disappearing around the curtain.

A tear formed at the corner of her eye and she brushed it away with an impatient hand. Well, what did she expect? That absence would make his heart grow fonder? She had to quit hoping for the impossible.

She turned onto her back and stared at the patch of ceiling above her bed. What was it he'd said when she'd mentioned a wife? *I guess I never found anyone interested enough in that position.* She couldn't believe that. There had to be lots of women in Gold Peak who would kill to be his wife.

Was she one of them? She didn't want to answer that question. She was too afraid of the answer. Not that it made any difference. He couldn't have made it any plainer if he'd put it into words. He was angry at her for leaving. But only his pride had been hurt. He'd never tried to get in touch with her those first lonely weeks in Phoenix, even though Mabel had her phone number and could have given it to him.

But he'd never asked. He hadn't cared enough. And she'd be a fool to go on hoping for something that could never happen. Maybe this fire was a sign for her to get out while her heart was still intact. Before she started kidding herself that the haunted look she'd seen in his eyes when he thought she wasn't looking meant anything.

She must have slept, since the next thing she knew a nurse was bending over her, shaking her gently by the shoulder.

"Ms. Matthews? How are you feeling?"

Ginny blinked sleepily at the round smiling face above her. "Better, I think. Thirsty."

"Here. Can you sit up?"

Ginny nodded and hauled herself back onto her pillows. She took the cup from the nurse and drank greedily until the nurse took the cup away from her.

"You need to take it easy on the water at first. We don't want you bringing it all back up again." The nurse popped a thermometer in her mouth then reached for her wrist and began checking her pulse. Apparently satisfied, she let her go and took the thermometer from her mouth. After peering at it for a moment she tucked it in her pocket then scribbled something on the chart above Ginny's bed. "Now," she said briskly, "can you manage some breakfast?"

"I think so." Ginny gingerly cleared her throat. "When can I leave here?"

The nurse reached for the curtain and dragged it back to reveal a large window. Sunlight bathed the pink blanket covering Ginny, making her feel even more determined to get out of that bed.

"The doctor will be in to see you soon. You can ask her then." The nurse disappeared, leaving her alone again.

Noises from the other side of the curtain told Ginny she wasn't alone in the room. She was glad the nurse hadn't pulled back the curtain separating the beds. She needed to be alone. To think.

She wasn't given much time to do that, however. Breakfast arrived, served by a nervous young girl in a pink striped uniform and no sooner had Ginny finished the scrambled eggs and bacon than a tall, willowy woman bustled around the curtain, uttered a brief greeting and reached for the chart above her bed.

Lines of weariness etched the doctor's brow as she studied the notes while Ginny watched anxiously. Finally the other woman lifted her head. "I'm Dr. Webster. I treated you last night when you came in. How do you feel?"

"Better." Ginny's voice cracked and she cleared her throat. "Well enough to go home."

The doctor frowned. "I understand you live in Philadelphia."

"Yes, but—"

"I really don't think you should be traveling just

yet. Give it a day or two, and give your lungs a chance to recover. You've given them quite a workout.''

''Well, I—''

''Is there somewhere you can stay for a couple of days? You have friends or family here?''

A vision of Cully popped into Ginny's mind. No, it was the last place she should be staying. ''I have a house in Gold Peak. I can stay there until I feel better.''

Dr. Webster seemed satisfied with that. ''Very well. I'll sign the release. I'll also write you a prescription for that throat. If you have any more trouble with your breathing, or the coughing doesn't go away in a day or two, I want you to come and see me again. All right?''

''I will. Thank you, doctor.''

''Wait for the nurse to help you dress.'' Dr. Webster moved to the curtain. ''You might feel a little light-headed at first, but that should pass.''

She disappeared and Ginny waited a moment or two before swinging her feet to the floor. The doctor was right. The floor tilted like the deck of an ocean liner. She sat down on the edge of the bed and took some deep breaths. That made her cough and she waited for the spasms to pass before getting unsteadily to her feet again.

At that moment a small dark-haired nurse appeared around the curtain. ''Ah, there you are.'' She beamed at Ginny. ''And here are your clothes.''

Ginny took the underwear, clean jeans and tank top from her in surprise. ''Where did these come from?''

''Your husband brought them in.''

For a nasty second or two Ginny's heart stopped beating. "My husband's dead," she said, her grating voice making her sound grouchy.

The nurse looked confused. "Oh, sorry. I meant the cute cowboy who brought you in last night. I thought he was your husband."

Fat chance, Ginny thought wryly. She was tempted to ask her what had given her such an idea but thought better of it. "No," she said carefully, "that was Cully Black. The county sheriff?"

The nurse laughed. "Oh, right. I thought he looked familiar." Then her face changed. "Oh, dear. I suppose I should tell you, he's waiting for you downstairs. I hope he's not... I mean you're not..." Her voice trailed off in embarrassment.

"He's not arresting me," Ginny said with a smile. "He's a good friend, that's all."

"Whew, I'm so glad. You don't look like a criminal." The nurse studied her with frank curiosity. "I heard you were in that motel fire in Gold Peak."

Struggling into her jeans, Ginny nodded.

The nurse shook out the pale green top, chattering happily as she waited for Ginny to take it. "It's all over the news today. Almost totally destroyed, they said. And you know the worst of it? They say someone deliberately set it on fire. Now who do you suppose would want to do a thing like that?"

Ginny's fingers suddenly felt too big and clumsy to zip up her jeans. Her mouth felt dry and she reached for the water.

"Probably a kid playing pranks, if you ask me," the nurse prattled on. "I really don't know what gets into the kids nowadays. All that violence on TV, that's what it is.''

Ginny swallowed a gulp of water and choked on it.

The nurse took the cup away from her and set it down. ''Are you all right? You look kind of pale. Maybe you should just sit here for a while and get your bearings.''

''No, I'm fine.''

She'd croaked the words and the nurse frowned. ''You don't look fine.''

Ginny forced a smile. ''Really, I am. Just drank too fast, that's all.'' *Why hadn't it occurred to her?* She'd assumed the fire was one of those nasty accidents that happen in motels and hotels sometimes. Someone falling asleep with a cigarette in his hand. Electrical faults. The building was old, it could have easily happened that way.

Only it hadn't. Someone had deliberately burned it to the ground. Someone who hadn't found what he wanted in her room? Someone who'd decided to get rid of her? *As he'd gotten rid of the Corbetts?*

''Well, if you're sure.'' The nurse still watched her, her eyes full of doubt. ''Wait there and I'll get a wheelchair.''

Ginny nodded, closing her eyes as the nurse disappeared around the curtain. The woman in the next bed was talking on the phone, apparently to her young son, reassuring him that she was all better and coming home in the next day or two.

Ginny felt a strong twinge of envy. How good it must be to have a normal life, where all you had to worry about was how well your kid was being taken care of while you were away.

All the while she was growing up she'd dreamed of excitement and adventure. That's what Cully had been at first…an adventure. Only she hadn't wanted the adventure to end. She'd wanted to take him with her, to share the excitement and the wonder of the world out there.

When he'd refused to go, she'd nursed her broken heart and stubbornly clung to her dream. When she'd married Brandon it had seemed that her dreams were coming true. She'd traveled the world with him, seen sights she'd only imagined in those childish dreams.

She'd sailed up the Amazon, climbed the Eiffel Tower. She'd flown over majestic snow-covered mountains and watched the sun rise from a vast, tropical ocean. She'd had excitement all right, enough to last her a lifetime.

Now this. This was excitement she could do without. Right now she'd gladly trade her life with the most boring life imaginable. *As long as Cully was in it.*

Shaken by the depths of her longing, she forced her mind off the subject.

"Here we are!" The nurse appeared around the curtain and beckoned to her. "Come on, get in the wheelchair. We don't want to keep Mr. Hunk waiting now, do we?"

Ginny managed a fake smile as she seated herself in the wheelchair. She felt like a fraud being pushed down the corridor to the elevator. She was perfectly capable of walking. In fact, she would have vastly preferred to be walking right then, instead of being wheeled into the lobby where Cully was leaning against the reception desk, chatting to the entranced young woman seated behind it.

Catching sight of Ginny, he straightened at once, his face creased in concern. "You sure you're up to leaving here?"

"Very sure." Just to prove it, Ginny shoved herself out of the wheelchair. "I can walk from here," she told the nurse, whose sole attention seem to be fixed on Cully.

"I'm supposed to wheel you outside," she said. "Do you have your car outside, Sheriff?"

"Yes, ma'am." Cully took hold of Ginny's arm, his warm grip giving her more comfort than she should feel. "I can manage from here."

"Well, if you're sure." Obviously disappointed, the nurse turned the wheelchair around. "'Bye, Sheriff. 'Bye, Ginny. Good luck."

She was going to need it, Ginny thought grimly as she walked unsteadily out into the warm sunshine.

After the clinical aroma of the hospital, the street stench of exhaust fumes and hamburgers from a nearby fast-food restaurant was almost welcome.

Cully supported her with his arm under her elbow as he led her to his Jeep. "Can you climb in or do you need some help?" he asked her when she eyed the vehicle.

"I can manage." Shaking his grip free, she reached for the door handle and hauled herself into the car. It bothered her how weak she felt, as if she'd been lying in bed for a week instead of a few hours. Not much longer, in fact, than she normally slept.

Cully rounded the hood of the Jeep and climbed up

beside her. "Okay, buckle up." He started the engine and obediently she fastened the seat belt at her hip.

"Thank you for bringing in some clean clothes for me."

"I had Lyla wash everything. Jed took them over to the ranch and brought them back here early this morning. Everything got pretty messed up in the parking lot, what with all the water and soot."

"Then I must thank Lyla. And Jed, too. That was sweet of them to go to all that trouble." She looked around. "Where's the rest of my stuff?"

"At the ranch." He slid a sideways glance at her. "Lyla's made up a bed for you. You can stay as long as you want."

Her heart skipped a beat. The thought of staying in that lovely house with him was tempting beyond words. Too tempting. "That's nice of you, Cully, but I don't want to put you and Lyla to all that trouble. I can stay at the Corbett house."

His mouth firmed in an expression that worried her. "I don't think so. I want you where I can keep an eye on you."

Now the fear was back, pulsing in its intensity. "You think someone tried to kill me."

"I don't know what to think." He pulled up at a stoplight, behind a shiny new BMW.

"The nurse told me the fire was deliberately set."

He seemed surprised. "News sure travels fast in this town. I didn't hear myself until a couple of hours ago."

"Do you have any idea who might have set it?"

"Not yet. The fire department in Rapid City's handling the investigation. From what I hear, someone did a pretty good job of it. Two whole cans of charcoal lighter fluid on the steps of that old building. It's amazing it stayed up as long as it did."

"Didn't the rooms have sprinkler systems? I thought it was the law."

"It is and they did." The car in front of them pulled away and he followed, glancing into his rearview mirror. "Whoever set the fire had gone to the trouble of turning them off."

In spite of the heat bouncing off the windows of the cab, she felt thoroughly chilled. "He really wanted me dead."

"Well, we still don't know that for sure." They had reached the highway out of town and Cully sped up.

Automatically Ginny peered into her side mirror. There was no sign of a gray minivan on the road behind them. "It's a little too much of a coincidence, don't you think? First my room searched, then the fire?"

"I'm not saying it isn't the same person. I'm saying you might not have been his first priority. If he was looking for something that could incriminate him in some way, and didn't find it, he might have figured he'd make sure nobody else did."

She thought about that. It didn't make her feel a whole lot better but it helped to know she might not have been the target of the fire. "I just wish I knew what it was he was looking for."

Cully uttered a harsh laugh. "If we knew that, we'd know where to start looking for him."

"What about the Corbetts' house? If he thought

whatever it was might be there, why didn't he burn that down, too?''

"It might not have occurred to him. After last night, though, he might get the idea in his head. Which is why, as soon as I've dropped you off at the ranch, I'm heading over to the house to check it out.''

"No.'' She sat up straight in her seat. "That will take you out of your way. You can drop me off at the motel and I'll pick up my car.''

"Your car isn't at the motel. I had Cory drive it out to the ranch. He came back with Jed.''

She thinned her lips. "You were taking an awful lot for granted.''

His sideways glance was sardonic. "I figured you'd give me an argument about staying at the ranch. The Sagebrush was the only motel in town. Where else are you going to stay? The doc says you shouldn't be flying for at least a couple of days.''

So he'd talked to the doctor, too. Was there no end to his interference in her life? "I could stay in Rapid City.''

"You could.'' He nodded affably. "But you're not going to. Not while there's someone out there who might want you dead.''

She had to admit, she'd feel a good deal safer with him watching out for her. "Well, all right. Thank you. Just for tonight, anyway. But you can't take me back to the ranch now. We need to go out to the Corbetts' house. Supposing the killer's there now, getting ready to burn down the house? He could just disappear and we'd never know who killed the Corbetts or why.''

"You can't go there with me. You just got out of the hospital. You need to take it easy.''

"I'm fine. All I have is a cough and a sore throat. We can't waste precious time going to the ranch first, Cully. You know that."

She could tell he was torn between doing his duty and worrying about her. The knowledge fueled her determination. "If we lose the chance of catching this guy just because you were being stubborn, how are you going to live with that? You have to go there now, Cully. You know you do."

Muttering a soft curse under his breath, he drove for a while without answering her. Then, just when she thought she'd have to urge him on one more time, he said firmly, "All right. But you stay right here in the car. With the doors locked."

Satisfied, she leaned back. The time to argue about that was when they got there. For now it was enough that she'd won the first round.

IF THERE WAS one thing that hadn't changed about Ginny, Cully thought, as he pulled up in front of the Corbetts' house a little later, it was that gutsy stubborn streak of hers.

After everything she'd been through the night before, in spite of the fear he'd seen in her eyes, she wasn't about to give up on finding the Corbetts' killer. Even though it seemed there was a good chance the same cold-blooded murderer could be after her, too.

He'd deliberately played down that angle of it. He didn't want to frighten her any more than was necessary. He had to admit, the way things were going, it looked as if Ginny could be in danger. What he should do was put her on a plane back to Philadelphia.

It bothered him how much he hated the thought of that. Once she left Gold Peak, he had a strong feeling she wouldn't be back. With the Corbetts gone, she had nothing left to come back for. Then again, if Ginny didn't want to leave, nothing he could do or say would make her go. That thought almost made him smile. Almost.

There was something else niggling at him. Something he didn't want to put into words. *Call me if you need me,* he'd told her. She'd been in mortal danger, yet he'd had to hear it from Cory, on his way to the fire. She could have died in that inferno. Without one word for him.

She'd always been like that, ever since he could remember. Even when she was small. *I can do it. I can manage.* They'd been her favorite words. She hadn't needed him then. And now, even when her life was threatened, she was still telling him she didn't need him. Well, he didn't need to be hit over the head to understand.

But there was one thing he wasn't going to argue about. As long as she was in his town, his county, his jurisdiction, he was responsible for her well-being. Whether she liked it or not, there was no way he would have let her stay in that house alone.

This was one time when Miss Independent wasn't getting her way. She'd have come back to the ranch for the night even if he had to carry her kicking and screaming all the way. All he could hope now was that once he got her there, he could keep his hands off her.

Chapter Nine

"You stay here," Cully ordered, as he climbed out of the Jeep. "Keep the doors locked, and if you see anything unusual, lean on the horn. I'll come running."

Ginny set her jaw. "I'd rather come in the house with you."

"I'm not going to argue about it." He stood on the ground, one hand poised to slam the door shut, his dark gaze warning her to mind what he said. "If someone is in the house, I don't need you getting in the way. This isn't a request, Ginny, it's an official order. Got that?"

Still she resisted, annoyed at his high-handed attitude. "And what about all the things Mabel listed in her will? I still have to collect those."

He drew his brows together across his nose. "You have the copy of the will with you?"

She held up her purse. "In here. But—"

"Give it to me."

She pressed her lips together.

"Give it to me, Ginny. We don't have time to stand and argue about it."

Deep down she knew he was right. If he had to deal with a cold-blooded killer in that house, she'd only be in the way. But she hated like hell having to sit there twiddling her thumbs, not knowing what was going on in there.

She sat for a moment longer while he stared at her in grim determination. Then, giving up, she snapped open her purse and pulled the folded papers from inside. "Try not to miss anything. I don't want to have to come back here."

He took the papers, calmly folding them up so he could tuck them in his pocket. "Don't worry," he said quietly. "I won't forget anything. I know how you feel about this house. And this town."

He didn't add, *and me,* but he might as well have uttered the words. She knew they were on his mind. She wanted to cry out after him, tell him how wrong he was. For all the good it would do.

She watched him stride up the path to the front door. Her heart pounded in apprehension. She didn't know what she would do if she heard a gun go off in the house. She'd have to call for help on his radio but then what?

The thought that he might be hurt—or worse—devastated her. She just couldn't sit there and let him die. She'd have to go in. No matter what he said.

Impatient with her runaway mind, she leaned back and tried to relax. If only she had something to read. Heaven only knew how long Cully would be in there, searching for broken windows, whatever. She should have told him to come and get her after he'd checked out the house. She could have at least helped him with collecting the bequests.

The minutes dragged by, while her impatience intensified, until she was grinding her teeth. To hell with it. The Jeep was heating up, even though the windows were down and it was parked in the shade beneath a bushy fir. Orders or not, she needed fresh air.

She unlocked the door and climbed down, her ears trained for any sound that might indicate the presence of another person. She was half expecting Old Man Wetherby to come wandering out of the forest again and the memory of Cully's words the night before drummed in her mind. *When a man's mind has gone, there's no telling what he's capable of.*

She shivered, her anxious gaze probing the shadowy woods for sight of the old man. Had Wetherby's mind snapped? Had he come gunning for Jim and Mabel? Was it his voice she'd heard in the basement, warning her she was going to die? The thought hadn't occurred to her before but now she wondered if perhaps the old man had followed her into the house and used the key to get into the basement.

Her skin prickled at the thought that he could have been pointing his shotgun at her in the dark down there. She hadn't mentioned the voice to Cully earlier because she'd been convinced she'd imagined it. Now she wasn't so sure. It could have been the old man. She should have told Cully. She'd have to tell him now.

Just in case Wetherby was watching her from the trees, she forced herself to stroll up the path. She didn't want to convey a sense of urgency and set him off if he was there. Part of her mind still insisted that she was being paranoid but after everything that had happened since she'd driven into Gold Peak, which seemed weeks ago now instead of a couple of days, she was ready to accept any possibility.

She paused at the front door and took another long look around. Luckily Cully had left it unlocked and she stepped inside the cool entranceway and closed the door gently behind her.

Standing at the entrance to the hallway, her gaze went immediately to the basement door. It was closed and she could hear no sound. No scraping, thumping or footsteps to suggest Cully was down there. He had to be somewhere else in the house.

Now that she thought about it, the silence was unnatural. If Cully had been doing an inspection as he'd said, surely she could have heard him? It was a big house but an old one. Floorboards creaked, hinges squeaked. Just yesterday she'd sat there listening to the roof popping and cracking in the warmth of the sun.

She paused, listening for any sound of someone moving around. Judging from the eerie silence, she might just as well be alone.

Her pulse flinched at the thought. Once more her mind raced with possibilities. What if the killer had seen them arrive? What if he'd attacked Cully from behind, before he'd had the chance to draw his gun?

Now that she came to think about it, she wasn't even sure Cully was carrying a gun. What if he were lying on the floor of the basement bleeding to death?

Unnerved, she called out his name. Her injured throat permitted no more than a hoarse cry that wouldn't have carried farther than the stairs.

She stared at the basement door, her heart pounding

with fear. She had to take a look. She couldn't just stand there letting her imagination scare her to death. She had to know for sure that he was all right.

Step by step she drew closer to the door, until she was within reach of the handle. Slowly she reached out and grasped it. To her relief, it turned and the door swung open with a loud squeak of the hinges.

She didn't want to go down there. The thought of descending the stairs into those black shadows, feeling her way to the floor until she could reach the light, made her want to throw up. Cully had said he'd get the power put on. But had he? Would she get to the bottom and find out the light wouldn't go on and she was in the dark?

She couldn't remember where she'd left the flashlight. In any case, she didn't have time to look for it now. Cully could be lying down there. *What if the killer was down there, too? Waiting for her?* She called his name in her thin, raspy voice that was no more than a hoarse whisper. Nothing moved.

Unnerved now, she backed away from the door and down to the light switch on the wall. She flicked it down and the bulbs in the hall lamps glowed. The extra light made her feel a little more secure. Leaving them on, she edged back to the door.

Now she could see down the steps right to the bottom, to where a pool of light spread out on the basement floor. Placing a foot firmly on the top step, she eased forward. One foot down, then another. Her knees felt so weak she wondered if they'd hold her up long enough to get down to the bottom.

The string dangled overhead as she reached the third step from the bottom. The musty smell of dust and mold seemed to fill her nostrils, irritating the tender lining of her throat. She longed to cough and dared not, though common sense told her that an intruder would already be alerted to her presence.

A faint crack made her jump with a violence that almost sent her forward down the rest of the steps. She paused, clinging to the unstable handrail that shifted under her grasp. It was only a floorboard above her head. Just the expansion of the old house again.

One more step and she could reach the string. Stretching out her arm, her fingers touched it, making it sway out of reach. Down one more step. Now she was half afraid to pull it, scared of what she might see. Taking a deep breath, she grasped the string and gave it a sharp tug.

Light bathed the oblong room, blinding her for a second or two. She blinked hard, squeezing her eyelids closed before opening them again. The room appeared to be empty. She pulled in a breath and let it out again, trying to relax her tense muscles. Just in case, she crept to the corner and peered carefully around it. The space in front of the window was bare.

It took her only a minute or two to check behind a pile of boxes, an ancient lawnmower, various garden tools and a large wooden chest that she knew contained the Christmas decorations. For a moment memory seared her mind as she remembered crowding around the Christmas tree with the rest of the kids, all eager to hang the ornaments on the fragrant branches.

Pushing the vision away, she took a last look

around and finally satisfied, headed back to the stairs. A quick tug shut her in darkness again for a moment. In her haste to reach the steps she brushed too close to a heavy shovel leaning against the wall. It fell with a clatter, jarring her nerves again.

Leaping for the stairs, she sped up to the welcome daylight beyond the door. Cully must be in the bedrooms somewhere, she decided with a wave of relief. Most likely sorting through Mabel's belongings to find the items listed in her will. Now she felt foolish and cursed her inventive mind.

Her mouth curved in a smile. Jim was always teasing her about her overactive imagination. Still smiling at the memory, she reached the top of the steps and through the open doorway.

She had taken only one step when without warning a muscled arm clamped around her chest, painfully crushing her breasts. Her assailant dragged her arm back and she was pulled hard against a sturdy body. She tried to scream as loud as her tortured throat would allow but the resulting gurgle was cut off by the large hand that descended over her mouth.

Instinctively she raised her knee and with every ounce of strength she possessed she rammed her heel backward. It connected with her attacker's shin with a loud crack.

His howl of pain rang in her ears and he released her. Finding herself free, she started to run headlong down the hall. One question pounded in her mind. *Where was Cully?*

Then, like a miracle, she heard his voice. "Ginny, wait! It's me, for chrissakes."

The voice, she realized, had come from behind her. Whirling around, she stared at him in disbelief.

He was bent over, one hand caressing his bruised shin.

"What the hell are you wearing?" he demanded. "Freaking spurs?"

Still shaking from the fright she'd had, she marched toward him. "Me? What about you? You manhandled me like I was some kind of punk druggie on a high. What the hell was that all about?"

"I thought you were the killer." He straightened, wincing as he shook his foot in an apparent attempt to ease the pain. "I thought I told you to stay put. What in blazes were you doing creeping around the basement like that? You were lucky I didn't shoot you."

"I was looking for you. I couldn't hear you moving around and I thought you might be lying on the floor down there."

"Yeah, well, sometimes you think too much." He leaned down to rub his sore shin.

He'd hit a button and she bristled. "What's that supposed to mean?"

Groaning, he straightened. "Aw, come on, Ginny. I didn't mean anything."

"Yes, you did." She stepped closer to him, shaking with the raw emotions that had suddenly rushed to the surface. Maybe it was the reaction after everything she'd gone through the past few months, maybe it was the effort of having to hold back so much anger, fear and frustration. Whatever it was, it was as if a seawall had collapsed, letting out a tide of uncontrollable passion. "I know what you meant! You think this is all my fault. If I hadn't left Gold Peak, Mabel and Jim would still be alive. You think I have something to do with all this, isn't that what you're thinking?''

His voice was a roar, sending her back a step or two. ''No, dammit, it's not what I'm thinking! Right now I don't know what to think. I do know that you're possibly in danger and it's up to me to protect you. I can't do that if you don't do what you're told.''

''Really! Well, this might surprise you, Sheriff Black, but I'm quite capable of taking care of myself. I don't need your precious protection.''

''The hell you don't.'' He reached her, grabbed her arms and gave her a little shake. ''I'm tired of listening to you brag about how self-sufficient you are. Seems to me you haven't exactly done a good job of it so far. You need protecting from yourself, Ginny Matthews. You always have.''

Furious, she tried to break free. ''Get your hands off me, Cully, or I'll—''

''You'll what?'' His dark eyes blazed at her, filled with such a strange mixture of fury, pain and longing that she was momentarily silenced. She could see the faint lines now, fanning away from the corners of his eyes, creasing his forehead, gouging his cheeks.

His warm hands held her in a strong grip that was more exciting than painful. His face was so close she could feel his warm breath brush her forehead. He smelled of soap and spicy musk, a heady fragrance that seemed to draw her closer, seeking the warmth of his body.

She forgot where they were and why they were there. She forgot everything that had happened since she'd left Gold Peak. The past came flooding back to engulf her and in that moment he seemed more powerful, more formidable, more masculine than she'd ever known him. And infinitely more desirable.

He must have seen something in her eyes, as his expression changed. For a breathtaking second their gazes clashed. Then his mouth was on hers and his powerful arms crushed her to him as if he were afraid she'd disappear if he let her go.

Closing her eyes, she returned his kiss, submerging herself in the sensual pressure of his hard body, the rough scrape of his jaw against hers, the electric thrill of his hands roaming her back, her waist, her midriff.

He buried his mouth in her neck and she shivered with the sheer pleasure of it. It had been so long, so very long. She turned her face, her lips searching for his. She could feel his breath, hot and fast on her cheek. She wanted him. Oh, God how she wanted him. His hand slid slowly up toward her breast and every nerve in her body begged him to touch her, ached for him to touch her.

Then the bubble burst as a sharp thud from outside broke them apart. Dazed, she stared at him, aware of his chest heaving with the effort to curb his weighted breath.

His head was tilted on one side, his expression sharp and wary. His hands held her, but now they were still and even as she registered that he let her go and drew back. "Sounded like a car door," he muttered then brushed past her and headed for the front door.

Trembling, she took a moment to compose herself. Her tank top was crumpled and pulled out of her jeans. Quickly, she tucked it back into the waistband and started to follow him to the door.

Cully paused as he opened it and looked back at her. "Wait here," he said, all traces of passion gone from his voice. "Wait here and do *not* come out until I tell you. Got that?"

She nodded and leaned back against the wall, trying to make sense of what had just happened. Where had all that passion come from? When had she ever felt so completely consumed by the longing that she couldn't even think straight? What the hell was the matter with her? Hadn't she learned anything from the past?

So caught up in the confusion boiling in her mind, it was some time before she realized that all was silent outside. Now the apprehension came creeping back. Cully had said it sounded as if someone had closed the door of a car. His car? Or someone else's car?

Burning with curiosity now, she hurried down to the front door. It wouldn't hurt to peek outside and try to see what was going on. She had almost reached the door when it flew open, startling her.

Cully stepped inside and she could tell right away that he wasn't happy. He'd jammed his hat down low on his forehead, shadowing his eyes but she could see his fierce scowl.

She moved closer to him. "Who was it?"

"I don't know. I didn't see anyone out there."

"Maybe it was Old Man Wetherby, snooping around your car."

"Maybe." His tone was clipped, guarded. "In any case, we'd better get that stuff for Paul. I left it all upstairs. Wait here and I'll get it."

She watched him take the stairs two at a time. Her stomach felt as if she'd swallowed stones. He was just going to ignore what had happened between them. That much was obvious. Well, she'd be damned if she'd mention it, either. If that kiss had meant so little to him, she'd make sure it never happened again. Ever.

The urge to feel the clean, fresh air on her face sent her outside. It was the same sun in the sky, the same pines circling the house, the same breeze shifting their branches. Yet everything seemed different somehow. The world had changed. She'd thought she was over Cully Black. But she wasn't. She was still in love with a man who liked her well enough to share his bed but not enough to share his life.

The door behind her slammed closed and Cully's boots scrunched on the hard ground behind her. "I put everything in here," he said, holding up her canvas bag. "I'll drop it off at Paul's office and empty it and then you can have it back."

She nodded, not trusting herself to speak. He sent her a brief glance, his face carefully neutral, then he opened the car door for her to climb in.

Without looking at him again she settled herself on the seat and stared stonily ahead as he pulled out in a wide circle then headed back down the rutted trail.

She was prepared to make the entire trip back to town in silence but as they turned onto the mountain road he fished something out of his shirt pocket and handed it to her. "Ever seen that before?"

She turned the plastic envelope over in her hand. It contained a thick gold earring. Examining it closer, she realized the design was made up of two snakes plaited together. "It looks familiar…" she paused, wondering where she'd seen it before. "Where did you find it?"

"On the floor in the basement." He flicked her a glance. "I went down there to check it out before I went upstairs."

"Oh." She concentrated on the earring.

"I was in the master bedroom when I heard you crashing around downstairs."

He'd sounded accusing. Annoyed, she said stiffly, "Well, excuse me for worrying about you. If you hadn't—" She broke off, her eyes widening. "I know where I've seen this before. At the Red Steer. The guy who waited on us was wearing one just like this."

"Luke Sorensen. Yeah, I thought so." He held out his hand for the envelope and she passed it back to him. "It couldn't have been there when the crime lab went over the place, or they would have found it."

"Which means he must have gone back later." She stared at Cully's rugged profile. "He could have been in the basement when I went back there. Maybe it was his voice I heard."

Cully gave her a sharp look. "You heard his voice?"

She nodded. "At the time I thought I'd imagined it. Then I thought it might have been Old Man Wetherby down there. But if Luke Sorensen went back there it could have been him."

"What did he say?"

"It was a whisper, that was all." She shivered. "He said I couldn't escape. That I was going to die."

Cully swore under his breath. "Why didn't you tell me that before?"

"I told you. I thought I'd imagined it."

"Well, it's time you sorted out what's in your imagination and what's real. From now on you tell me everything, whether you think you imagined it or not. Got that?"

"Got that," she said, without bothering to hide her resentment. "But what I don't understand is why Luke Sorensen would threaten me. As far as I know, we've never met."

"Most likely he was just trying to frighten you so you'd leave the house."

"Well, he succeeded in that." She frowned. "I wonder what he was doing there. Do you think he set the fire at the motel?"

"I don't know," Cully said grimly. "But I sure intend to find out." He was silent for a moment, staring hard at the road ahead, then he added quietly, "Look, I'm sorry about what happened back there at the house."

Her pulse skipped a beat. She knew instantly what he meant and waited until she was sure she could sound indifferent.

"There's no need to apologize."

"Yes, there is. You were...we were...upset. I guess I took advantage of that. I—"

Suddenly angry again, she said swiftly, "Just forget it, Cully. It didn't mean anything. It's like you said, we were upset, that's all. It was just one of those stupid things."

Her heart beat so hard in the silence that followed she was sure he could hear it. Then, with just a trace of bitterness he said, "Yeah, you're right. It was stupid."

She felt like crying. She seemed to do a lot of that

lately. And that was stupid, too. She'd wasted far too many tears over Cully Black. It was time she quit, once and for all.

Cully drove fast through the mountain curves but she paid little attention to where they were going. A vague feeling that she had forgotten to tell Cully something important kept niggling at her but she was too miserable to care what it was.

Slumped in her seat, she failed to notice the vehicle creeping up on them, until Cully swore and a second or two later a sharp bump sent them swerving to the right.

She yelped with fear as the wheels of the Jeep slid dangerously close to the side of the road. Less than three feet of gravel separated them from the edge of the mountain, beyond which the ground fell away in a steep drop.

Cursing, Cully wrestled the wheel and straightened the lurching Jeep. Ginny peered over her shoulder, just in time to see the vehicle draw level with them. Its tinted windows wouldn't allow her a clear view of the driver but there was no mistaking the gray mini-van. Now there was no doubt left in her mind. She hadn't imagined anything. The van was real.

Her relief was short-lived as the van swerved into them again and once more Cully had to fight the wheel. He braked hard, swinging them around in a crazy circle, kicking up dust and pebbles as the Jeep bucked and skidded across the road.

They hit the mountainside and bounced off and the back of the Jeep fishtailed as they came out of yet another skid. Ginny uttered a hoarse cry as the edge of the mountain came up fast. She shut her eyes, hung onto her seat and prayed.

The Jeep's tires squealed in protest, then she was thrown forward as they came to an abrupt stop. The engine died and the silence that followed seemed overpowering.

She waited until she could get her lungs working again then cautiously opened her eyes. They were on the very edge of the mountain.

Ahead of them the taillights of the minivan were just disappearing around a curve in the road. Cully reached for his radio and started talking rapidly into it. She heard Jed's answering voice but was too shaken to take much notice of what he said.

Finally Cully turned to her and now she could see the strain etched on his face. "They should be able to pick him up on the highway."

She nodded and looked down at her hands. They were locked together and she pulled them apart. "I—" Her voice cracked and she tried again. "I wasn't imagining things after all."

"No," Cully said, his voice hard-edged. "I guess you weren't."

"Are we…how close are we?"

He glanced out of his window. "About an inch or two from the edge. Thank God for four-wheel drive."

"Amen." She pulled in a deep breath. It was time to voice the fear that had been intensifying ever since last night. "I guess it's true. Someone is trying to kill me."

He avoided her gaze. "Looks that way."

"You think it's the same person who killed the Corbetts."

"I'd say it's a pretty safe bet."

"Do you think it was Luke Sorensen?"

"It could be, I guess."

She stared out at the road ahead. "I just wish I knew why."

After a pause, Cully cleared his throat. "Well, if Jed and Cory do their job, we should soon find out." He started the engine. "Let's get out of here."

She held her breath while he slowly backed away from the edge of the road, her tension mounting again as they rounded the first curve. "You don't think he's waiting for us, do you? I mean, he could block the road or something. He could shoot us."

"I think if he wanted to shoot you he would have done it by now. Or at least tried. I'd say he's trying to make it look like an accident."

"He's not being very subtle about it." She leaned forward to get a better look at the road as they rounded another bend. "First he ransacks my room, then sets fire to the motel, then tries to run us off the road. Surely he must know that if he'd succeeded, no one is going to accept that it was an accident?"

"Exactly. Which means we're dealing with an irrational person." Cully frowned. "He's acting on impulse. Taking advantage whenever he can."

Ginny breathed a sigh of relief as the highway came into view without any sign of the minivan. "Isn't every murderer irrational?"

"It depends. Most of them are controlled and devious. They plan everything down to the last detail. The irrational ones are the toughest to figure out. There's no pattern to follow. I guess you could—"

He broke off as his radio chattered. After listening

to Jed's voice again for a while he said, "All right. I'm coming in. I'll see you in the office in a few minutes." He replaced the radio, while Ginny anxiously watched his face.

When he said nothing, she said impatiently, "Well? What did he say? Did they catch him?"

Cully sighed. "It looks like he gave them the slip. He must have turned off somewhere before he hit the highway."

Ginny stared at him in dismay. "But where would he go? There's only one road off this mountain. Unless he…"

"Doubled back," Cully finished for her. "He must have pulled behind a rock until we passed and then headed back up. He could be anywhere on the mountain by now."

The fear was now full-blown, drying out her mouth, chilling her body, muddling her mind. Helplessly she looked at Cully's grim face. "So now what do we do?"

"I guess," Cully said slowly, "we go back to square one."

Chapter Ten

"First," Cully said, as he eased the Jeep back onto the road, "I'm going to check out a few things. I'll drop you off at the Red Steer and you can catch up with Sally. You should be safe there."

Startled, Ginny stared at him. "But what if Luke is there? What if he tries to—"

"If Luke tried to run us off the road, he'll most likely be skulking around on the mountain some-where. If not, he'll be working out at the quarry on his day job. Even if he was driving the minivan, he's not going to try anything in front of everyone. He's been taking too much trouble to try and make it look like an accident."

She did her best to feel reassured by that. "So what will you be checking out?"

He seemed reluctant to answer but after a long pause he said, "Among other things, I'm going to find out more about the accident that killed your husband."

Her fingers curled in her lap. "You still think someone sabotaged his plane?"

"Like I said, anything's possible. I still think there

could be some connection, though I can't figure out what it could be. I want to talk to Luke, if I can find him and Ben Wetherby, as well, though I don't think that old man had anything to do with all this.''

After all the excitement, her head ached too much to struggle with the puzzle right then. She closed her eyes and leaned her head back against the seat. All this stress was taking a toll on her.

She wished now that she'd stayed in Philadelphia and had never come back to Gold Peak. Right now she'd be in her office, going over brochures and samples of the spring line with nothing more to worry about than the rapidly changing tastes of the buying public.

She wouldn't be running scared, afraid for her life and she wouldn't be going through all this agony over a man who didn't appear to have a clue about love and commitment. She'd be safe, both physically and emotionally.

The thought was so appealing she was tempted to drive her rented car to the airport and leave this town behind her forever.

Except she couldn't do that. Not now. Someone had killed her beloved foster parents and was trying to kill her, too. She couldn't leave until she knew why. She had to trust Cully to solve the puzzle and give her back her peace of mind. Even if she had to spend another ten or so years trying to forget him again.

Several minutes later Cully pulled into the parking lot of the Red Steer and let her out. ''I shouldn't be more than an hour or two. I want you to stay put until I get back. Can you promise me that?''

Ginny nodded. At least it was better than *Got that?* "I'll have some lunch while I'm here. What about you? When will you eat?"

"I'll grab something later." He studied her, his gaze so intent her heart skipped a beat. "Take care of yourself, Ginny. Don't do anything stupid."

Before she could answer, he slammed the door and roared off.

She shook her head at the retreating Jeep, then headed for the swing doors of the tavern.

The clamor of voices striving to be heard above the jangling music of dueling guitars threatened to deafen her as she made her way to the long bar at the end of the room. Apparently business at the Red Steer was still as brisk as ever at lunchtime.

Curious stares followed her as she threaded her way through the tables and now and then a familiar face greeted her, warily, as if the owner wasn't sure how she'd respond.

She recognized Neil Baumann, who lifted a hand to wave at her. The man with him gave her a hard stare as she waved back and she guessed they'd be talking about her as soon as she was out of earshot. No doubt discussing her relationship with the sheriff of McKewen County, she thought wryly. She just hoped Cully knew what he was doing, inviting her to stay at the ranch. The town gossips would have a field day with that.

Reaching the bar, she shouldered her way between two burly workmen, who immediately gave her plenty of space. A nervous glance in both directions reassured her. Luke was nowhere to be seen.

The blond woman behind the bar sent her a brief glance, then demanded, "So what'll it be?"

Ginny managed a weak smile. Raising her wispy voice to be heard above the racket behind her, she said, "We used to share a beer together in the old days, but that was before I worried about my waistline. I think I'll take a diet soda instead."

The woman's chin shot up, blue eyes stared at her for a second or two, then a huge grin split her mouth wide open. "Ginny Matthews! I heard you were back in town!"

The men on either side of Ginny stared at her as if she'd sprouted horns.

Ignoring them, Ginny said hoarsely, "What time is your break?"

Sally Irwin sent a longing glance at the clock. "Not for another hour. Can you stay that long?"

She'd been pretty much ordered to, Ginny thought wryly. "Sure, I'll take a chicken sandwich and a salad. That will keep me busy for a while."

"Go find a table." Sally waved a hand at the crowded room. "I'll bring it over to you." She grinned again. "It's sure good to see you, Ginny. We've got a heck of a lot of catching up to do."

Ginny nodded in response and picked up her soda. It was hard to believe she'd been so much a part of this place all those years ago. She'd spent practically every Saturday night here and countless lunch hours, too.

Everything in the place was as familiar to her as her own apartment, from the wagon wheel chandelier hanging from the center of the ceiling to the wooden menu holders on the burn-scarred tables.

That's what was different, she realized, as she seated herself at a midget-size table for one near the fireplace. No stink or haze of cigarette smoke. She wondered what it had taken to persuade the owners to go non-smoking.

Sally brought Ginny her lunch, promising to be back as soon as she could get off. "Luke's not here," she said, when Ginny casually asked about him. "He doesn't come in here for lunch. At least I've never seen him. He works here on my night off, and comes in occasionally for a beer." She narrowed her eyes. "I didn't know you two knew each other."

"Oh, we don't," Ginny assured her hastily. "I met him the other night when I was in here with Cully."

"Yeah, I heard about that." Sally gave her a lusty wink. "I gotta run, but get ready to spill the beans when I get back." She hurried off, leaving Ginny to wonder exactly what it was Sally had heard.

Having long finished her lunch, Ginny was glancing through a copy of the local newspaper she'd found lying at a nearby table when Sally finally joined her.

She'd brought two glasses of Chablis with her, and set one down in front of Ginny. "We can't celebrate a reunion without a drink," she said, drawing a chair up to the minuscule table. "Here's to old times."

Ginny touched glasses with her and took a sip of her wine. The room had just about emptied out and the noise level was appreciatively lower.

Before she could speak, Sally leaned toward her, asking eagerly, "So tell me. *Everything.* I heard you were caught in the Sagebrush fire last night. Didn't you have to spend the night in the hospital?"

Ginny nodded. "I'm all right now, though. Except for a sore throat."

"Yeah, sounds like it really made a mess of your voice. Sounds good, though." She leaned forward and nudged Ginny's arm. "It's all husky and mysterious. Sounds sexy. You should keep it like that. By the way, someone said you were married, and someone else said you're a widow." Her face creased in concern. "I hope they were wrong."

Ginny set her glass down carefully on the table. "Actually I am a widow. My husband died three months ago."

Sally uttered a cry of dismay. "Aw, geez, I'm sorry. What a bummer. Was he sick for long?"

"It was an accident," Ginny said hurriedly. "So tell me about you. You look great, by the way."

Sally's round face broke into a grin. "Yeah, fat and sassy, that's me. Never could keep the weight off." Her gaze flicked over Ginny. "Not like you. Skinny as a telephone pole. Don't know how you do it." She reached for her glass. "So, what's with you and Cully?"

Ginny avoided the other woman's gaze. Only Sally had known the true depths of her feelings for Cully and how hard it had been to leave town without him. "We had some business to discuss," she said, trying to sound indifferent. "The Corbetts left me the house, you know."

"Yeah, I heard." Sally's grin vanished. "Terrible what happened to them. I still can't believe it. No one can. We've never had a killing in Gold Peak before. Shook us all up real bad. Then the fire at the motel last night...'' She peered at Ginny. ''You are okay, right?''

Ginny smiled. ''I think so. Just shaken up, that's all.'' She glanced at Sally's ringless left hand. ''You're not married?''

''Divorced.'' Sally shook her frizzy bangs out of her eyes. ''Who isn't these days?'' She glanced around the room, then leaned forward and in a loud whisper announced, ''I've got a boyfriend, though.''

''Really?'' Ginny coughed and took a sip of wine to soothe her throat. ''So what's he like? What's his name? What does he do?''

Sally's wide grin reappeared. ''His name is Dave. David Petersen, and he's a sales rep. He goes around recruiting people to sell stuff in their homes.''

''What sort of stuff?''

''Fitness stuff. You know, bicycles, rowing machines, weight machines, all kinds of stuff. There's this one machine he has that's supposed to take inches off your thighs....'' She launched into a complicated explanation of the machine, while Ginny did her best to stay interested.

''He's a great guy,'' Sally said, when she'd finished describing the new marvel. ''We've only just met, but he's *so* attentive. All the time asking where I'll be and what I'm doing. Wants to know every little detail. Says he worries about me.'' She let out her hearty laugh. ''Nobody ever worried about me before.''

''He sounds very nice.''

She laughed. ''He's a sweetheart. The other night I went into Rapid City to see a movie with my neighbor and Dave wanted to know where we'd gone, who we saw, how long it took us to get there. I haven't had a man that interested in what I'm doing since Jim waited for me at the front door when I was coming home from a date. I like it. Makes me feel protected, you know?''

"That's nice," Ginny murmured. Although she didn't say so, Sally's words had disturbed her. Listening to her friend talk about her boyfriend had reminded her of Brandon. Like Sally, at first she had taken his interest in her activities as concern for her welfare, until she'd married him and found out just how cruel and manipulative that interest could be. She could only hope that this David person wasn't the jealous, possessive kind. If so, Sally was in for a lot of heartache.

"I thought I'd lost him last night," Sally said, grabbing Ginny's attention again. "He was staying at the Sagebrush, like you. Luckily it was the first floor. Got out with everything, thank God. He spent the rest of the night with us. I told him he could stay with me and the kids tonight, too, but he's got a schedule he has to keep to, so he took off early this morning."

Ginny stared at her in delight. "You've got kids? How old?"

"Gary's seven, and Lisa's nine, going on thirty." Sally wrinkled her nose. "I don't blame Dave for not wanting to spend the night with us. The kids can be a bit of a handful. I get the feeling he's not used to being around kids."

"You must not see much of him," Ginny said carefully, "if he's traveling around all the time. Where does he live?"

"I'm not sure. Somewhere in Nevada, I think. He

doesn't talk much about himself. Say,'' she grabbed Ginny's hand, ''why don't you and Cully join Dave and me for dinner next week? I'm meeting him in Rapid City. We're going to that new restaurant. Harrington's or something. Oh, that's right, you wouldn't know it, but I hear it's real grand, lots of good food and soft music.'' She flung her hand at the speaker above her head. ''Nothing like this lousy stuff.''

Ginny looked at her in surprise. ''I thought you loved country music.''

''That's when I was young and stupid. You might not think it to look at me, but my tastes are a lot more sophisticated now.'' She sat back and beamed at Ginny. ''I watch ballet and travel movies on TV, and I'm learning yoga.''

Wondering who she was trying to impress, Ginny smiled. ''Well, thanks, but I don't think I'll be here next week. I'm flying back to the east coast in a couple of days.''

Sally raised an eyebrow at her. ''What are you doing there?''

''I live there.''

''I thought Mabel said you lived in Phoenix.''

''I did.'' Ginny cleared her throat. ''I moved to the east coast…when my husband died.'' It wasn't the truth, of course but easier than having to explain exactly why she'd moved across country.

''That's too bad.'' Sally's blue eyes filled with sympathy. ''You must be lonely.'' She paused, then added slyly, ''You know Cully's never married.''

Ginny dropped her gaze and reached for her wineglass. ''So I heard.''

"Don't suppose there's any chance of you two hitching up together again?"

Aware that her laugh sounded forced, Ginny cleared her throat again. "Can you see Cully living in a city as big as Philadelphia?"

"No," Sally said firmly, "I can't. Cully loves his job and his horses and his ranch too much to leave. But what's to stop you from living here?"

Ginny shook her head. "I'm not the same Ginny who left Gold Peak twelve years ago. I've changed. Too much to live in a town like this again."

"Well, you ain't changed that much. You always did want to get out of here." Sally drained her glass. "Guess some people just can't stomach small-town living. Shame. I always thought that you and Cully belonged together."

The ache in Ginny's heart was so acute she couldn't look at her old friend. "Well, that just goes to show," she murmured, "you can't judge people by appearances."

She changed the subject then, steering the conversation back to Sally's children. But the ache stayed with her and she had the feeling that it would linger for a long, long time.

CULLY SAT BEHIND his desk, listening to the ceiling fan whirring gently above his head. One hand held the phone to his ear, while the fingers of his other hand drummed impatiently on the desk. Nothing irritated him quite as much as being put on hold, especially when he was conducting an investigation.

Finally the line clicked in his ear. "Sheriff Black," he said, when a harsh male voice announced he was

Fred Owens. "Did Luke Sorensen come into work today?"

Fred verified that Luke worked at the quarry.

"Is he still there?"

Cully frowned at the answer. Luke Sorensen had been in the quarry since seven that morning. "You're sure?"

"Quite sure," Fred assured him. "I saw him arrive and I saw him again when I took some supplies out there a little while ago."

"Do you know what he's driving?"

"He comes in on a mountain bike." The voice paused. "Did he do something wrong? The bike's his. He's had it a long time."

"Yeah, I know. I just thought he might have been driving something else today."

"Nope. The bike's right here. I can see it from this window."

"Well, thanks." Cully was about to put the phone down when Fred asked, "You want me to get him?"

"No, forget it. It's nothing. Don't even tell him I called." He dropped the receiver in its cradle, then sat staring at it for minute. No, dammit. Luke had been at the house when he had no business to be.

Cully pushed his chair back and grabbed his hat. There was only one way to find out why. He had to go up to the quarry and talk to him.

Twenty minutes later he pulled into the stony trail that led to the quarry. Battered pickups and dusty sports vehicles littered the space in front of the scruffy trailer where Cully assumed he'd find Fred Owens.

The foreman turned out to be a bear of a man with a full beard and a belly that hung over his belt. He

looked up when Cully stuck his head in the doorway
of the makeshift office. The place stunk of cigarette
smoke, stale beer and sweaty bodies. He couldn't
imagine how anyone could stomach that all day.

"Sheriff Black," he said, fixing the big guy with
a stare. "I'd like a word with Luke Sorensen."

Fred shoved himself up from his chair, tilting it
back against the wall. "What's he done? I don't allow
no lawbreakers on my jobs. If he's broken the law
he's out."

"As far as I know he hasn't done anything." Cully
backed away as Fred's huge body filled the doorway.
"I just want to ask him some questions, that's all."

Fred looked as if he would argue but then apparently changed his mind. Waving his hand at the area
behind him he said, "You'll find him back there. Ask
one of the guys to give him a shout."

Cully nodded his thanks, then made his way across
the sun-baked ground to where the massive crater
scarred the hillside. In earlier days the land had been
mined for gold but now the quarry provided much of
the material used on construction sites in the area.
Cully had always had mixed feelings about the work
done there. The materials were badly needed for a
growing town but he hated what it was doing to the
countryside.

Catching sight of two men deep in conversation,
he asked for Luke. A few minutes later the young
man climbed up to where Cully waited. He seemed
uneasy and kept sending glances over to his work-
mates as he approached.

Cully reached into his pocket and withdrew the envelope. "Recognize this?"

Luke's hand moved to his left ear. "I dunno," he mumbled. "What is it?"

Cully reached out and touched the earring in Luke's right ear. "I'd say it was the twin to this one."

Luke's face reddened and his gaze shifted to the ground. "Yeah, well, maybe it's mine."

"Yeah? Well, guess where I found it."

Luke scraped the ground with the toe of his boot. "I dunno. I lost it somewhere."

"You lost it in the Corbetts' house." Cully dangled the envelope in front of him. "I'd say I've got a pretty good case of breaking and entering, probably burglary, and possibly murder."

Luke's chin shot up, his eyes blazing with fear. "I didn't kill no one. I swear I didn't. And I didn't take nothing that wasn't promised me. And that's the truth."

Cully tucked the envelope back in his pocket. "So what did you take?"

Luke stared down at the ground again. "I took Jim's old guitar. Weren't worth nothing anyway. He promised me I could have it soon as I learned to play properly. Then he went and got himself killed, and I figured the guitar was mine."

"So you decided to break in and steal it."

"I didn't break in. The door was unlocked. I went in, got the guitar from the basement and left. I didn't take nothing else. I carried it up on my shoulder. It must have caught against my earring somehow and broke it."

"And you didn't see anyone else while you were there?"

Luke looked surprised by the question. "No, no one was there. The house was empty."

"What about outside? See a car? A van?"

"I told you, there was no one there. Just me."

"When was this?"

"I dunno." He lifted his face to the sky and squeezed his eyes shut. "Sunday morning. Three days ago. Yeah, that was it."

"You're sure about that?"

"Yeah, it was Sunday morning."

Cully frowned. *The day before Ginny arrived in town.* If she'd heard a voice in the basement, it wasn't Luke's. Neither did it seem that Luke could have been driving the minivan that morning. "All right." Cully gave him a stern look. "You and I are going to have a long chat about this guitar business. Later."

He spun around to leave and Luke called out after him, "I didn't steal it. It was promised me."

Ignoring him, Cully kept going. The sense of urgency that had plagued him ever since that morning was now a clanging warning in his head. He needed to get back to Ginny. And from now on, he wasn't letting her out of his sight.

Chapter Eleven

Cully arrived at the Red Steer just as Sally was getting ready to leave. Ginny saw him push through the doors and immediately forgot everything else. Like a thirsty traveler finding water, she couldn't seem to stop gulping in the sight of him.

Aware of Sally staring at her, she hastily switched her gaze but the damage had been done.

Sally grinned and said softly, "Let me guess. Cully Black just walked in."

Ginny sighed. "Okay, so I'm glad to see him. I've been sitting here for almost two hours. Much as I like this place, and talking to you, I'm ready for some fresh air."

"Uh-huh. Or a fresh cowboy, right?"

Ginny managed a light laugh. "You haven't changed a bit, Sally Irwin."

"Thank the good Lord." Sally glanced over her shoulder at Cully, who had stopped to speak to a couple of men at a table a few yards away. "I got to admit, girl, you know how to pick 'em. I've often wondered how come some young chick hasn't pounced on our good-looking sheriff and put a ring on his finger. As my poor dead momma used to say, he's one fine specimen of a man.''

"I guess Cully just isn't the marrying kind.''

"I think you're right. More's the pity. What a waste. What a damn waste.'' Sally raised her voice as Cully moved toward them. "Well, there you are, Sheriff. This little gal here has been chomping at the bit wondering where you were.''

Ginny squirmed as Cully's intent gaze rested on her face. "Sorry. Took longer than I'd figured.''

"That's okay,'' Ginny said lightly. "Sally and I have been having a great time catching up on all the gossip.''

"We sure have. And now I gotta go. I need to spend some time with my kids when they get out of school before I have to come back here and face the mob again tonight.'' Sally pushed her chair back and stood. "So I'll leave you two alone.'' She slapped Cully's arm. "Behave yourself, cowboy. Take good care of my friend, here.''

"I intend to.'' Once more his gaze flicked over Ginny's face, sending all kinds of thoroughly unsettling signals. He turned back to Sally. "You take good care of those kids of yours. I saw Gary just the other day. That boy is growing like a weed.''

"Ain't he, though.'' Sally gave him her expansive grin. "Costing me a fortune in clothes, too. Now he's talking about them fancy sneakers all the kids are wearing. A pair of them cost more than a week's groceries, I swear. I'll have to get another job at this rate.''

Still laughing, she headed for the door, stopping

now and then to exchange a snappy word or two with the few customers that were left.

"She hasn't changed a bit," Ginny said, as her friend disappeared out the doors. She rose from her chair and gathered up her purse. "I can't believe it's been more than ten years since I last saw her. It seems like yesterday."

"Twelve," Cully said. He stood back to allow her to move past him.

She glanced up at him. "Pardon?"

"It's been twelve years since you left."

Once more he'd unsettled her. Wondering just what his point was, she started moving toward the door, just as he added quietly, "And it seems like a life-time."

She was still trying to figure out exactly what his remarks had meant as they pulled out of the parking lot in the Jeep, heading for the highway.

She thought about asking him but was wary of making something out of nothing. The memory of that kiss this morning still hovered between them. She could sense the restraint in him, as if he were wary of saying the wrong thing, of misleading her by some stray word or action.

Her skin tingled when she thought about being in his arms again. In fact, throughout her conversation with Sally, the memory of it had kept coming back to torment her. How could she be this close to him and not remember his hands on her, his mouth hun-grily searching for hers?

He'd agreed, a little too readily, when she'd called it stupid. But in those brief moments she'd sensed the heat in his kiss, the longing that matched her own. If that car door hadn't slammed outside the house, who knows what might have happened.

So it was just as well they had been interrupted. Had they gone any further and finished what they'd started, all those feelings she'd worked so hard to suppress all these years would have come roaring back, only to end in heartbreak again. No, she'd been hurt enough by his indifference. She would never give him the chance to do that to her again.

Casting about for something to say, anything to take her mind off her insistent memories, she said lightly, "I'd like to pick up something for dinner tonight. I thought maybe we could stop by the store on the way through town."

He didn't answer her right away but seemed intent on watching the road. "Lyla's most likely got the meal all planned out," he said finally. "Better not get in her way. She figures the kitchen is her castle."

"I wasn't going to get in the way," Ginny said mildly. "I just thought it would be nice if I cooked dinner and gave her a break."

"I reckon she'd like that." His smile went a long way to calming her rattled nerves. "Take a raincheck?"

She nodded, wondering if she'd be around long enough to cook dinner for him. "So, tell me what happened. Did you talk to Luke?"

"I did. He was working at the quarry all day. The guys out there backed him up on that."

She waited a moment then asked casually, "What about the plane crash? Did you find out anything about that?"

"I'm still waiting for them to get back to me with

a report on that.'' He braked as a silver sports car cut in front of him. They were passing the burned out motel and an involuntary shudder shook Ginny's body. One end of the building was completely collapsed, with only a skeleton frame left standing.

The other end, where she and Marty had climbed down the ladder, was a blackened hull with shattered windows and a charred roof. The stench of burned wood and acrid chemicals still filled the air.

Someone had set that fire deliberately. Someone who wanted her dead. If Brandon could see her now, he'd certainly have the last laugh. It was as if he'd kept his word and reached out from the grave. *If you have the guts to outlive me, I'll come right back to haunt you. You will never be rid of me. Never.*

''You okay?''

The question, spoken in Cully's deep voice startled her. ''I'm fine.'' She unclenched her fingers and forced a smile. ''I was just thinking about the fire, that's all. I could have died in there.''

His face was set in stone as he answered her. ''No one's going to hurt you, Ginny. I'll make sure of that. You're safe as long as you are with me.''

She had no answer to that. Part of her was comforted by his concern and his assurances. The other part of her longed for something more than just a cop doing his duty. More than just a man responding to his basic urges. Much, much more.

''I was thinking we might take a ride up to Wetherby's place. I need to talk to him, and we can check on your house one more time before we call it a day.''

It seemed strange to hear it referred to as her house. She still couldn't accept the fact that she owned it.

All she knew was that she didn't want go back in there again. Twice she'd been scared out of her wits and now she seemed to sense an undercurrent of something frightening, something evil in that house.

Even the memory of Cully's searing kisses that morning had failed to disperse the sense of impending doom. She could only hope that the house would sell quickly and that she would never have to go back there again.

"Is that okay with you? I can take you back to the ranch first if you don't feel up to it."

His voice reminded her she hadn't answered him. "No, of course I'll go with you. I feel just fine. Really."

He gave her a searching look that seemed to penetrate her soul. She dropped her gaze, wondering if he could see in her eyes what was so potently obvious in her mind and her body. He was inches away. If she moved just slightly to the left, she could lean against him, feel the warmth of his body.

A vision flashed into her mind. Two naked bodies, glistening with sweat, locked together while their hunger took them to a blazing, tumultuous climax. Mouths devouring each other, hands reaching, stroking, touching, trembling with the wonder of a passion never imagined until that moment.

"On second thought, maybe it's not a good idea to take you up the mountain again. Whoever tried to run us off the road could still be up there, waiting for another chance. You've had enough excitement for one day. I'll take you back to the ranch first. You'll be safer there."

"No!" She turned to him and placed her hand on

his arm. "I want to go with you. I don't want to be alone. You said yourself I'll be safe as long as I'm with you." Part of that was true. And part of it was the growing awareness that soon she would have to leave him and go back to her life in Philadelphia. She needed to make the most of the time she had left with him, even if that meant facing danger with him.

"You won't be alone. Lyla will be there, and the dogs."

"Please, Cully." Her fingers curled on hard muscle. "I really want to go with you."

After a long pause, he said quietly, "Okay. I just hope I don't live to regret this."

Worried that he might change his mind, she started talking about her lunch with Sally, hoping to get both their minds off the risk of driving up the mountain again.

Even so, she found herself watching the road behind them through her side-view mirror, afraid that any minute she'd see the gray minivan looming up behind them.

They reached the trail to her house without seeing another vehicle, however, and she began to relax a little as they pulled up in front of the yard.

It took all her willpower to walk into the house with Cully. He made her stay close behind him while he quickly checked the rooms and then ordered her to stay in the hallway while he went down into the basement.

"It's all clear," he told her as he came back up the stairs. "I thought the driver of that van might have come back here, but nothing seems to have been disturbed since we left, so I'm hoping he's given up on whatever he hoped to find here.''

"Good, then I guess it will be all right for Neil to show the house? He's waiting for your approval before bringing anyone out here.'' She followed Cully outside, breathing a good deal more easily once the door was closed behind them.

"I guess we should hold off a little longer,'' Cully said, climbing back into the Jeep. "I want to make sure that no one's using the house to hide from the law. Someone out there apparently has a key to this place, and until we find out who that is, I don't want strangers walking around.''

Ginny gasped. "Darn, that's what I meant to do. I need to get a locksmith out here to change the locks.''

"We'll do it on the way back through town.'' Cully looked at his watch. "We should have time to talk to Wetherby and still get back to town before the locksmith closes.''

Ginny looked back at the house as they pulled away. Strange that the one place where she'd always felt safe and secure should now feel so frightening and hostile. With any luck at all, she'd never have to set foot in it again.

Wetherby's shack sat deep in the woods, beyond a rough trail that ended several yards from the ramshackle building. The urgent barking of a large dog greeted them as they made their way on foot through the tangle of undergrowth to where the shack stood in a small clearing.

Ginny was very glad she had Cully's sturdy body in front of her as they approached the rickety porch, where an angry rottweiler stood, feet apart, hair bristling on his back as he snarled a warning at them.

Cully paused, his hand resting on his holster as he shouted out, "Ben? Ben! It's the sheriff. I want a word with you."

The dog growled, deep in his throat, then erupted into a frenzy of barking as the door opened and Old Man Wetherby appeared in the doorway, his shotgun slung over his arm.

"Shut *up,* Max!" he yelled. "Whadda you want, Sheriff?"

"I want to talk to you." Cully took a couple of steps forward, then paused as the dog snarled again. "You wanna put that beast on a leash?"

The old man put his hand on the quivering animal's back. "Get inside, Max." When the dog didn't move, Wetherby gave it a hefty shove. "I said get *inside, dammit.*"

With a final warning growl deep in its throat, the dog turned and slunk through the doorway.

Wetherby closed it behind him then faced them again. "That you, Ginny Matthews?"

Ginny stepped out from the shelter of Cully's broad back. "Hi, Mr. Wetherby. Yes, it's me."

The old man scowled at Cully. "What's she doing here?"

"She's looking for the key to her house." Cully took a few steps closer to Wetherby. "You don't happen to have it, do you, Ben?"

"Key? Heck, no, I don't have no goldarn key. Whadda I wanna key to that house fer?"

"I dunno." Cully lifted his hands in a shrug. "I

thought maybe you were looking for something. Down in the basement, maybe?''

The old man looked bewildered. ''I ain't never set foot in that house. Not when Jim was alive, nor now that he's a dead'un. Not once. I wouldn't go in that house if you paid me a million dollars, that's fer sure. Butch's ghost is right there in that dang house. I'm not going near that place. No sir.''

''You told Ginny that you'd seen the ghost of your dog,'' Cully said. ''Now what I'm wondering, Ben, is how you happened to see that ghost if you didn't go in the house.''

Wetherby's pale blue eyes remained steadily on Cully's face. ''Well, I'll tell ya, Sheriff. I seen that ghost through the window. At night. Ol' Butch is a'wandering around there, happy as a duck on a pond. I seen his shadow moving down that there hallway as plain as can be.''

''And you didn't go in there after him?''

''Hell, no! Whadda you take me fer, an idjet? Like I told you, ain't no way I'm going in that house.'' He raised his shotgun and shook it at Cully. ''This'n here gun ain't no damn good against no ghost, and thassa fact. Thought you'd 'a known that, Sheriff.''

Cully nodded. ''Reckon I do at that, Ben.'' He twisted his head to take a look around. ''You didn't happen to see a minivan around here, did you? A big old gray van?''

Wetherby's eyes narrowed. ''I might have done.''

Ginny caught her breath. ''It has tinted windows,'' she blurted out. ''You know, the blue kind that you can't see through?''

Wetherby's head swung on her direction. ''You

shouldn't be up here, Ginny Matthews,'' he said, his voice carrying across the clearing. "You don't belong here now. Go back where you belong.''

"Ginny owns the Corbett house, Ben." Cully sent her a warning glance. "She has as much right on the mountain as you do.''

"Nope, that she don't. That house don't belong to no one except Butch now. That blamed bastard Jim Corbett killed my dog, and now Butch has the whole house to hisself. Ain't no one gonna live there no more. So go on home, Sheriff, and take Ginny Matthews with you. She don't belong up here.''

"I will Ben, just as soon as you tell me about that gray minivan you saw. Did you get behind the wheel? Maybe take it down the mountain for a joyride?''

Wetherby's blue eyes widened. "Me? I ain't driven nothing but my ol' Ford over there for the last ten years.'' He jerked his thumb at the battered pickup parked at the side of the shack. "Damn near gets me where I want to go and thassa fact.''

Cully jammed his thumbs into the pockets of his jeans. "Then I reckon you won't mind if I take a quick look around here, then?''

Ginny held her breath as the two men faced off. Wetherby still held the shotgun pointed at the sky, while Cully stood with his feet braced apart, his body tensed for action.

After what seemed an eternity, the old man shook his head. "Hell no, Sheriff. You look wherever you want. But I'm telling you there ain't nothing here but my ol' truck.''

Cully jerked his head at Ginny to follow him as he

tramped around the shack, searching the ground as he went.

Ginny waited until they were out of earshot before asking urgently, "Do you really think he was driving that van? And set the fire?" The chill ate into her bones again. "And killed the Corbetts?"

"Well, he seemed pretty determined to get you off the mountain." Cully paused, then dropped to his haunches to stare closer at the ground. "But his growl is a whole lot fiercer than his bite. I don't think that old man is capable of murder, no matter how mad he was at Jim. I can see him maybe shooting out the windows of the house, but shooting them both in cold blood and then running them off the road in their truck takes a lot more than temper. It takes an evil mind, not to mention muscle. No, I don't think Ben Wetherby's our man."

"Then what are you looking for?"

Cully got to his feet. "Tire tracks. Even on dry ground, a van that size would leave some tracks. Even if Ben didn't commit the murders, there's always the possibility he's involved with the killer in some way."

The icicles slid down Ginny's back. "Are you saying he hired someone to kill Jim and Mabel?"

"No, he doesn't have that kind of money. But he may know more than he's telling us. I'll have Cory bring him down to the station. Ben's more likely to talk if he feels threatened by his surroundings."

They had reached the other side of the shack and Ginny followed him out into the clearing. Wetherby still stood on the porch, but now the shotgun rested on the floor, leaning against the wall, while the old man attempted to light a pipe, the match's flame shielded by his gnarled hand.

"Find anything, Sheriff?" Wetherby's gaze probed Cully's face, while smoke from the pipe wreathed about the old man's head.

Instead of answering him, Cully approached the porch and set one foot on the bottom step. "Where'd you see the van, Ben? Was it around the Corbett house?"

The old man's shrewd gaze never faltered. "Don't remember where I saw it. The memory's not what it used to be, Sheriff."

Cully nodded. "Well, maybe you'd remember better if you came down to the station."

Wetherby jumped as if scalded. Snatching the pipe from his mouth he spluttered, "I ain't going into town, no way. If there's anything you want to ask me, you can ask away right here."

"The van," Cully said patiently. "Where did you see it?"

Wetherby crammed the tobacco into the pipe's bowl with his thumb. Ginny winced, wondering how he did that without scorching his skin.

"Maybe I did see it near the Corbett house," Wetherby muttered. "Parked under the trees, it was. I thought it was strange, but I didn't go near it. I mind me own business. Live longer that way."

"Did you see who was driving it?"

Ginny held her breath as the old man stuck the pipe in his mouth and puffed away for several agonizing seconds before answering. "Nope," he said at last. "Couldn't make out if'n there was anyone in it. Couldn't see through them dark windows."

"How long was it parked there?"

Wetherby shrugged. "Can't really say. It was there when I walked down there to check my traps, and it was still there when I left."

"And when was this?"

"This morning. Right about dawn, I reckon."

Cully stepped back. "Well, I'd be obliged if you keep an eye out for it. If you see it again, you give me a call, okay?"

Wetherby nodded and reached for his shotgun. "Sure will, Sheriff."

Cully turned back to Ginny. "Okay, let's go. We need to get back to town before that locksmith closes."

Ginny waved to the old man but he turned away without acknowledging her.

"Don't let him bother you too much," Cully said, as they walked back to the Jeep. "He's a little muddled in the head, and sees anyone connected to the Corbetts as a threat."

"That's not a very comforting thought."

Cully opened the car door for her. "I still believe he's harmless, but I wouldn't come up here on your own until we get this thing settled."

Ginny shivered as she slid onto the seat. "Don't worry, I have no intention of coming back here. I've put the house in Neil's hands now, and he can deal with it. Once it's sold, I'll have nothing else to do with it."

He gave her a look she couldn't interpret but didn't comment on her remark. Instead he changed the subject and talked instead about his ranch in an effort, Ginny suspected, to get her mind off her problems.

They reached town without incident and Cully parked in the recently built strip mall. "I have to run by the office," he said, as Ginny climbed out. "It will only take a minute or two and by the time you're done here I'll be back. Just wait for me inside the shop, okay?"

"Okay." Ginny slammed the door shut and hurried across the parking lot to the little office that housed the locksmith. She felt vulnerable without Cully's reassuring presence by her side. Vulnerable and lonely. Something she would have to get used to when this was over, she reminded herself grimly as she entered the stuffy little office.

The man seated behind the desk raised his head. "Can I help you?"

Quickly she told him what she wanted and waited while he fussed with the form he wanted her to fill out. When she was done she fished out her credit card from her purse. "I'll pay you ahead of time," she said when the locksmith looked surprised. "I don't know how long I'll be in town. The new keys will go to Neil Baumann. He's selling the place."

The man took the card from her and finished the transaction. The whole thing only took about five minutes and Ginny wandered to the door to look out into the parking lot. There were no more than a dozen or so vehicles parked there and no sign of Cully's red Cherokee.

She could feel the locksmith's gaze on her back, no doubt wondering why she didn't leave. She didn't want to tell him that Cully had asked her to stay in there until he got back. That would have raised more questions than it answered.

Try as she might, she couldn't think of anything to ask the man that would delay her leaving. Finally she gave up and opened the door, letting it close gently behind her.

He'd said he would be back in a few minutes. She was standing in a strip mall, with people walking about. Not a very big mall and not that many people, true but surely enough that no one would try anything out there in broad daylight.

Trying to feel reassured, she wandered down to the travel agent's office and studied the posters of Europe and Hawaii in the window. Something reflected in the glass caught her attention. Certain that she was mistaken, she swung around to take a look.

It was sitting just yards from where she stood. She couldn't imagine why she hadn't noticed it before. Maybe because it had been mostly hidden from the angle of the locksmith's office.

There was no mistaking the dented license plate, the gouged passenger door. It was the same gray minivan that had been following her. The same van that had almost run her off the road.

Frantically she looked around for Cully's Jeep. *Where was he?* He'd said a few minutes. He had to be there any minute. Maybe she should call him. The locksmith must have a phone. She'd call from there.

She spun around to rush back to the locksmith's office. As she did so, she caught sight of a familiar figure hurrying out of the beauty shop across the parking lot. It was Sally Irwin and she was heading toward her.

Despite her urgency, Ginny didn't want to ignore the woman. She was about to raise her hand and give her old friend a brief wave before diving into the locksmith's office when Sally came to an abrupt stop.

Ginny froze, unable to believe her eyes as Sally calmly unlocked the door of the gray minivan and climbed into the driver's seat. Stunned, she could only stand and watch as her longtime friend and former soul mate drove past her in the van that just that morning had almost sent her and Cully to their deaths.

Chapter Twelve

In his office, Cully was trying to make sense of the information he'd just been given by the FAA investigator on the phone with him. All along it had been thought that Brandon Pierce had been alone in the plane when it crashed. Now it seemed that someone else could have been in there with him.

"If the body in the plane was burned beyond recognition," Cully asked, "how did you identify Brandon Pierce?"

"The county sheriff's department was responsible for that." The clipped voice paused, then added, "Hold on, I have the report here somewhere." Again Cully waited and finally, the investigator returned. "Yeah, here it is. Looks like they just assumed the identity."

"No matching of dental records or DNA?"

"Nope. A plane crashed and burned, solo pilot, single remains found on board, records showed Pierce was the pilot. Unless there is evidence of a crime scene and in the absence of a missing person's report, a rural investigation would probably rest on the assumption of identity, since there was nothing to indicate otherwise. The body was burned in the fire, so no one could visually identify it. I guess they'll change their minds now and do a proper investigation.''

"So all they had was the ring and the watch to go on.''

There was a long pause, then the voice said carefully, ''There's no mention here of a ring or a watch. Just what was left of a watch, that's all.''

Cully frowned. "Wait a minute. Are you telling me they didn't find a wedding ring or an engraved watch in the wreckage? Are you real sure about that?''

"Positive. I took down the report myself. Not much survived the fire. What little was left would have been listed here in the report.''

Cully thanked him and hung up. He could hear Ginny's voice clear in his mind. *He told Jim that Brandon was dead and that all that was left of his belongings were his wedding ring and the watch I'd given him for an anniversary gift. My name was on the back of it.*

If the ring or the watch hadn't been found in the wreck, how would an investigator know about them? He wouldn't, which meant that the man who called the Corbetts wasn't an investigator. He was the killer. He must have taken the ring and watch off Brandon Pierce before setting fire to the plane. That's how he'd made the connection to Ginny. Her name on the back of a watch. They weren't dealing with an amateur, that was for sure.

A few minutes later, Cully pulled into the strip mall and spotted Ginny right away. She stood on the edge of the sidewalk, staring across the parking lot as if she'd seen the ghost of Ben Wetherby's dead dog.

Annoyed with her for ignoring his demands that she stay put until he got back, he parked in the space right next to where she stood, cut the engine and swung himself out of the Jeep. "I thought I told you—" He got a good look at her face then and broke off. "What's the matter? What happened?"

She turned to him, her voice hushed with shock. "Sally. She was driving the minivan. The one that tried to run us off the road."

Disbelief rippled through him. "Are you sure? Sally Irwin? You're sure it's the same van?" He paused, struggling to absorb this latest surprise. "Wait a minute. Sally was driving her blue Mazda. I saw it today outside the Red Steer."

"It was Sally." Ginny looked as if she were about to burst into tears. "She got into the van and drove it away. I saw her. She was over there." Her hand shook as she pointed across the parking lot.

"And you're quite sure it's the same van?"

"Yes. I saw the dented license plate. I'd know that van anywhere. It's the same one, Cully. I can't believe it. Why would Sally want to hurt me?"

"I don't know," Cully said grimly, "but I'm sure as hell going to find out." He looked at his watch. "She's probably on her way back to the Red Steer. Let's go ask her. Though if she did try to run us off the road, I can't believe she'd be driving the van around town for everyone to see."

"It was the same van, Cully. You've got to believe me."

She had ahold of his sleeve and all the common

sense in the world couldn't stop him from putting his arm around her. "Come on," he said gently. "We'll stop by the office and call Lyla, tell her to put dinner on hold, and then we'll go to the Red Steer, have a beer or two, and find out exactly what Sally has been up to, okay?"

She nodded, her eyes so trusting and full of fear, his heart twisted inside of him. Just let him get his hands on whoever was doing this to her and he'd come down so hard the bastard would wish he'd never been born. Or she. Cully heaved a sigh. He just couldn't believe that Sally was involved in all this. Especially in view of the report he'd just received.

Deciding to keep that information to himself for the time being, he drove back to his office and put in the call to Lyla.

The housekeeper was disappointed that she'd miss seeing Ginny. "I was planning on leaving early," she told him. "My granddaughter is in her school play tonight. I promised her I'd be there."

"That's okay," Cully assured her. "You go ahead. Ginny and I can grab a bite to eat at the Red Steer."

"You're sure? I've put Ginny's things in the blue room. If she needs anything else…"

"Quit worrying, will you? I'll take care of everything. You just go and enjoy your granddaughter's big moment." He replaced the receiver and glanced at Ginny. She sat staring at a map on the wall above his desk, though he was quite sure she didn't see a thing on it. "Looks like it's steak at the Steer again tonight," he said. "Lyla's got an important date."

She looked at him as if she hadn't heard a word he'd said. The urge hit him so hard and so fast he was helpless to resist. He rounded the desk and hauled her against him. "Listen to me," he said fiercely. "Nothing's going to happen to you. I'll make sure of that. You have to trust me, okay?"

"I do trust you."

The whisper had barely left her lips before he covered them with his own. She clung to him and he closed his arms around her, his body responding at once to the firm pressure of her breasts against his chest.

Ever since he'd kissed her in the Corbett house, he'd longed to do it again. Man, how he wanted her. He wanted to take her right now back to the ranch, throw her on his bed and bury himself in her tempting body. He kissed her as he'd never kissed anyone before—hot, searching kisses that she returned with an urgency that matched his own.

She was all passion in his arms, thrusting against him as if she couldn't get close enough to satisfy her. There were too many clothes in the way. He wanted to rip them all off, to feel once again the soft, smooth touch of her bare flesh against his.

He reached for the hem of her shirt, pulling it free from her jeans. Eagerly she helped him, her own hands tugging at his shirt. Heat raced through his veins to pound in his head, chasing away all doubt, all common sense.

Then, unbelievably, the shrill peal of the phone shattered the moment. Ginny jumped back, one hand covering her mouth as she backed away from him. He gave her one last desperate look then reached for the phone.

"Sheriff? It's Jed. We got trouble on the mountain. It's Ben Wetherby. He's been shot."

Still dazed, Cully blinked hard. "He's dead?"

"Close to. He's in the hospital in Rapid City. In a coma. Doc says he doesn't know if he'll make it."

"Did he say anything?"

"Nope. Neil Baumann found him when he went up to look around the Corbett house. Ben was lying unconscious in the front yard. Took a while to get an ambulance out there to pick him up. Crime lab's out there now."

Cully rubbed the back of his hand across his eyes. "All right, let me know if they find anything. And stay by Ben's side. If he wakes up, try to get as much out of him as possible. Then call me. I'll either be in the Red Steer or at home."

"Will do." Jed paused then added, "What's going on, Cully? Have we got a serial killer on the loose in Gold Peak?"

"I sure as hell hope not. I think Ben might have seen more than was healthy for him. Let's just hope he wakes up and can tell us what went down."

Cully hung up the phone and turned to Ginny.

She stared at him, white-faced, her hands clutching her upper arms. "What?"

"Ben Wetherby." He could see no way to spare her this. "He's been shot."

"Oh, no." She covered her face with her hands. "How many more before this is over? It's all my fault. I should never have come back here."

"Hey, don't talk like that." He grabbed her shoulders and gave her a little shake. "We're in this together now, you hear me?"

Her lovely eyes were troubled as she looked up at him. "I don't want anything to happen to you. Or anyone else. Maybe I should just leave and go back to Philadelphia."

"You think you'll be any safer there?" He reached for his hat and crammed it on his head. "Forget it, Ginny. You're not leaving my sight until we figure out how to find this nutcase and put a stop to all this." He took hold of her arm and led her unresisting to the door. "The first place we're going is to the Steer and talk to Sally."

"You don't think—"

"No, I don't." No matter how bad it looked, he couldn't picture Sally Irwin as a cold-blooded killer. "I'm just hoping she can help us figure out what's going on."

Ten minutes later they pulled up outside the Red Steer. As Cully cut the engine, he heard Ginny gasp. Following her gaze he saw what had caught her attention. A dusty, battered gray minivan with tinted windows. If it wasn't the van that had battled them on the mountain then it was its twin.

He pulled in a deep breath. "Try to act as normal as possible," he warned Ginny as they walked side by side toward the doors of the tavern. "We don't want to tip off Sally before I'm ready to ask the questions."

"I'll try." Ginny looked defeated, as if she'd given up on everybody and everything.

"Hang in there, sunshine," he told her. "We'll get to the bottom of this, I promise."

That raised a faint smile. "I'd forgotten you used to call me that."

He hadn't forgotten. He could still remember how he'd felt whenever she'd walked into a room. As if the sun had lit up the whole place. The aching memory made him wince.

They reached the doors and he held one open for her to enter. The usual babble of raised voices, strident laughter and the thudding beat of country music greeted them as he followed her into the crowded room. This was the Steer's busiest time, when weary workers dropped in to relax over a beer before making their way home at the end of a long day.

Sally bounced around behind the bar, taking orders and exchanging friendly barbs with the customers. Cully sat Ginny down at an empty table and then made his way toward the thirsty group leaning against the bar, all anxious to get their hands around a cold beer.

He caught Sally's eye and within a minute or two she paused in front of him. "Nice to see you, Sheriff. What'll it be?"

He ordered a beer and a glass of wine then added, "Can you give me a minute or two over there?" He jerked his thumb to where Ginny sat anxiously watching him.

Sally followed his gaze. "Sure. Soon as I get a chance. What's up?" Her eyes widened in apprehension. "Not one of my kids, is it?"

Cully shook his head. "Nothing like that, so you can quit worrying about them."

She looked relieved. "Thank God. I've got good baby-sitters, but you never know these days. I'll be over as soon as Wally can manage on his own." She tilted her head at the bartender busily filling glasses at the end of the bar. "I want to talk to you, anyway, Sheriff. I wanna report a robbery."

"Hey, Sally," someone yelled. "How much longer are you gonna keep us waiting?"

Sally grimaced. "Better go. I'll get over there as soon as I can."

Cully picked up the drinks and carried them back to the table where Ginny sat with her elbows on the table, her chin in her hands. "Sally'll be over in a minute," he told her as he placed the glass of wine in front of her. "We'll order dinner then."

"I'm not hungry." She reached for her wine and took a hefty sip of it.

"You shouldn't drink on an empty stomach," he reminded her. He lifted the beer glass to his lips.

"Neither should you."

His wry grimace softened her haunted features. "I didn't say do as I do, I said do as I say."

She nodded. "Just like a man."

Relieved that she seemed calmer, he kept the conversation light, all the time scanning the room for anything out of the ordinary.

Fifteen minutes went by before Sally finally scurried over. Ginny had just left to visit the ladies' room, giving him the chance to question Sally alone.

"I don't have time to sit," she said when Cully gestured to the empty chair. "What is it you wanted?"

He got straight to the point. "I was wondering where you got that van you're driving."

Sally scowled. "That's what I wanted to talk to you about. That scumbag of a salesman stole my car. He was supposed to have left town this morning, but he was still in the house when I got home this after-noon.''

Cully raised his eyebrows in mute question and Sally made an impatient gesture with her hand. ''Boy-friend. Or so I thought. Name's David Petersen, works for some fitness company selling exercise ma-chines. Anyway, he was in the motel last night when it got burned out, so he spent the rest of the night at my place. He was supposed to leave this morning, but when I got home he was still there. He must have stolen the keys to my car out of my purse while I was in the bathroom. Next thing I knew he'd gone and so was my Mazda. Good thing for me he left the keys to that old clunker in the ignition, or I wouldn't have gotten here tonight.''

She paused for breath as Cully pulled his notebook and pen from his shirt pocket. He scribbled down the few bits of information Sally had given him then looked up at her. ''I'll put out an APB for the car. What's the license number?''

She told him, adding a few curses for good mea-sure.

''Anything else you can tell me about him? What does he look like?''

She held a hand up above her head. ''This tall, good-looking, real thick light brown hair, brown eyes, kind of thin.''

''Any distinguishing marks?''

''Not that I can think of.'' Sally swore again. ''Should've known he was too good to be true. What a damn fool I was.''

''Did he say where he lived?''

''Somewhere in Nevada. Near Reno, I think. Never

talked much about himself.'' Her face darkened. ''Bet he was freaking married.''

''Did he say anything about himself that might help track him down?''

She screwed up her face in an effort to concentrate. ''Can't think of anything.'' A shout from the bar turned her head. ''If I do I'll sure as heck let you know.'' She glanced up as Ginny appeared at her side. ''You two want something to eat?''

Ginny shook her head but Cully said firmly, ''Bring us a couple of steak dinners. Medium rare.''

''You got it.'' Sally rushed off and Cully tucked the notebook back in his pocket.

Ginny sat down opposite him, her eyes full of apprehension. ''Well, what did she say?''

Cully filled her in on Sally's story. ''Looks like Sally's boyfriend is the man we're looking for,'' he added when he'd finished.

Ginny looked at him, bewilderment plain on her face. ''Sally told me about him just this morning. She was so excited about him. But who is he? Why does he want to hurt me?''

''You've never heard of a David Petersen?''

She shook her head.

Cully sighed. ''I wasn't going to tell you this until later, but I got the report back on the plane crash that killed your husband.''

Her eyes widened. ''And?''

Hesitating, he drummed his fingers on the table, then said abruptly, ''Brandon Pierce filed a flight plan, stating he was flying solo. But someone at the airport swore he saw another man climb into the plane with him before he took off from Phoenix.''

Ginny frowned. "I don't understand. When they found the plane…"

"They found the remains of only one person. Your husband."

"Then who was the other man? Why didn't they find him?"

"That's what I'd like to know." Cully leaned back in his chair. "But I'd take an even bet it's David Petersen."

Ginny's fingers curled around her glass. "You think he killed Brandon."

"I think it's possible. It wouldn't be that hard to land a small plane in a field somewhere remote, kill your passenger and set fire to the plane, making it look like it crashed, then hike out of there back to town."

"But Brandon always flew his own plane. He'd never let anyone take over the controls."

"He could have been forced down at gunpoint."

"But why? Why go to all that trouble?"

"It's a good way to cover up a murder. The killer was most likely figuring on the plane never being found. If it hadn't been for a surveillance pilot looking for drug dealers on the Canadian border, your husband's body might have been there for years before someone spotted the wreckage."

Ginny's face registered her surprise. "Canada? What was Brandon doing that far north? I assumed he'd crashed in Idaho."

"Not according to the report I got. He went down in Montana." He paused, studying her face. "Are you absolutely certain you haven't heard the name before? Someone your husband might have known?"

"Brandon didn't have many friends. He had two business partners, and an assistant, but no one by the name of David Petersen."

"Look." He leaned forward, willing her to work with him. "Supposing Brandon Pierce was mixed up in something. He was an engineer, flew his plane all over the country. Traveled extensively abroad, right?"

"Yes, but—"

"Wait a minute. Hear me out. Just suppose he was involved in something big. Drug dealing, for instance. That's big time and there's some pretty mean players out there. Maybe Brandon got greedy, wanted some of the profits himself and upset the big guys. So they got rid of him. Probably figuring that by the time someone found his body, there'd be nothing left to tie him in to them."

"But even if that were true, and I find that very hard to believe, what does that have to do with me? I left Brandon six months before he died. I had no contact with him after that."

"But you were still a strong connection. Maybe you can identify the bad guys. Or maybe they're just covering all their tracks. The Corbetts were the one connection left between you and your husband. If someone, say David Petersen, wanted to track you down, the Corbetts would be the logical place to start."

"But why did he have to kill them?"

"Same reason he's after you. Because they could identify him. If something happened to you, they'd know who was trying to find you. Once he was sure they couldn't tell him where you were, they'd no longer be useful to him.''

When she spoke, her voice was barely above a whisper, and he had to lean in close to hear her. ''So he killed them, then he sat and waited for me to turn up.''

''Probably figuring on you coming home for the funeral.'' She was silent for a long moment, apparently turning everything over in her mind. Then she said sadly, ''And now poor Old Man Wetherby.''

''Yeah.'' Cully felt a surge of anger. ''He must have seen Petersen skulking around the Corbett house. I reckon Petersen thought he'd killed the old man, though I'm kind of surprised he just left him there instead of hiding the body. Might have been in too much of a hurry to do anything else with it.''

''So now what do we do?''

Her fear was palpable. He could see it in her eyes, in the slight tremor of her hand as she lifted her glass and drank deeply from it.

''We track down Petersen. We have the license number of the van, though it's probably stolen. We know he's driving Sally's Mazda. Or at least, he was. He could have stolen something else by now.'' He peered at his watch. ''Looks like it's going to be a long night.''

Sally chose that moment to return with the steaks and he was pleased to see Ginny eat, even if she did leave half the meal on her plate. Deliberately he changed the subject, asking her about her job, her life in Philadelphia, anything to keep her distracted.

When they were finished eating he asked for a doggie bag and Ginny actually smiled as she piled the remains of her steak into it.

"Rags and Puddles are gonna be your friends for life," he told her, as they walked out to the Jeep. Seeing her nervously glance around the parking lot, he put an arm about her and pulled her close. The craving was still there, eating at his gut. Once this was over, he promised himself and everything calmed down again, he would do something about it and to hell with the consequences. Right now he had work to do.

Back at the office once more, he switched on the desk lamps, softening the harsh atmosphere of the room. He offered Ginny a sports magazine to read but she shook her head.

"I'll just sit here and watch." She settled herself on the hard chair and tried to look comfortable.

His mouth twisted in a wry smile. "I'll be as quick as I can." Seating himself in front of the computer, he switched it on and waited impatiently for it to warm up.

Ten minutes later, he had what he wanted. The van did belong to a David Petersen, salesman for Softline Sports, Incorporated, and he lived in Carson City, Nevada. A few minutes later, Cully was calling the man's house.

The woman who answered him sounded weary, as if she'd been woken up from a deep sleep. He glanced at the clock. It was only a little after nine. "My name is Sheriff Cully Black," he told her, "McKewen County, Oregon." Before he could ask for Petersen, she interrupted him with a cry. "You've found him? Where is he? Is he all right?"

Cully frowned. "Excuse me, ma'am?"

The voice faltered. "Oh, I'm sorry... I thought..." her voice trailed off.

"I wanted to speak to David Petersen. Is he there?"

"No." Now the voice sounded resigned. "He's not. I'm Madeline Petersen. His wife."

Cully was getting a nasty feeling in the pit of his stomach. "Ma'am, can you tell me where he is?"

There was a pause, then the woman said shortly, "I've answered all these questions, before, Sheriff. I don't know where my husband is. He's been missing for over a week now. No one seems to know where he is. If you're not calling to tell me you found him, why *did* you call?"

"This *is* the David Petersen who works for Softline Sports?"

"For the past fifteen years. Yes. And if you're suggesting that he just up and left me, well I can tell you, you're wrong. I know what they say about traveling salesmen, but David was different. As I told the other officers, we were happy. We were planning on celebrating our tenth wedding anniversary next month..." She paused, apparently struggling to control her voice "...in Hawaii."

Cully tapped his fingers on the desk. "I'm sorry, ma'am. I'm sure everyone is doing his best to find your husband."

"Yeah, that's what they all say."

The click in his ear effectively put an end to the conversation. Cully hung up and sat frowning at the phone.

"Well?"

For a moment he'd forgotten Ginny was there. He gave her a reassuring smile. "Well, he's not in Nevada."

She didn't return his smile. "I gathered that much. So he's married. Poor Sally."

Cully swung his chair around to face her. "David Petersen, traveling salesman for the same company for fifteen years. Married happily for ten and about to celebrate with his wife in Hawaii. Does that sound like a cold-blooded murderer?"

Her eyes widened. "No, it doesn't. But—"

He lifted his hand. "Wait. Let me make some calls." He spent the next few minutes on the phone, aware of Ginny's gaze fixed on his face as he talked. Finally he hung up and turned to her. "According to the police report in Nevada, Madeline Petersen reported her husband missing five days ago. He always calls her every evening when he's on the road. She had an itinerary of his route. When he didn't call the third evening, she started calling the motels. He never made any of them."

"Except the Sagebrush."

"Which wasn't on his itinerary."

The fear was back on her face. "Are you saying what I think you're saying?"

"I guess I'm saying that the man who stole Sally's car is probably not David Petersen."

"Then who is he?"

"Guess we're back to square one on that. The point is, Sally has the real David Petersen's minivan."

"Oh, no." She stared at him, her face growing pale. "So if this man isn't David Petersen, he must have stolen the van from him."

"And Petersen is missing."

Her eyes widened. "He killed him?"

"It's beginning to look that way." He climbed to his feet, his body tense with frustration. "Right now we're both tired. It's been a long day. Maybe Ben Wetherby will wake up and be able to tell us more. In the meantime, I'm going to get you back to the ranch so you can get some rest."

He reached for her hands and pulled her to her feet. "I know how you must feel." He pulled her close and wrapped his arms around her. Resting his chin on her silky hair he added softly, "We'll find him. Don't worry. Sooner or later he'll make a mistake and we'll get him."

Her voice was muffled but he understood her words and they chilled him as nothing else had done. "I just hope," she said with a note of desperation, "that you get him before he gets me."

Chapter Thirteen

Except for the glow from the porch lights, the house was in darkness when Cully parked outside it later. Ginny could hear the faint barking of the dogs inside, a sound that reassured her as she waited for Cully to unlock the heavy door.

Even so, he made her stay on the porch with the dogs standing guard while he went inside and checked all the rooms. Nervously waiting for him to return, she fondled the animals' ears. Their exuberant greeting lifted her spirits. For now she was safe and could put her fears behind her for the night.

Cully returned to let her into the house and she followed him inside. As he closed the door behind her, her jitters intensified. She wasn't sure if it was a reaction to everything she'd been through that day, or the fact that she was alone with Cully in his house.

Last night Lyla's presence had acted as a buffer between them. Even if things had threatened to get complicated, there wasn't a lot they could have done about it.

But the situation had changed drastically since then. She could still feel the demanding pressure of his mouth on hers, his hands on her body with an urgency that had her smoldering like a lit fuse. All the way back to the ranch she'd fought the images in her mind, trying to ease the tension that seemed to hover between them like a force field, humming with emotions too powerful to explore.

They had said little to each other on the way back, each deep in their own thoughts. She would have given a month's pay to know what he was thinking.

The prospect of spending the night alone with him both excited and worried her. The possibility that they might end up in bed together was foremost in her mind, yet now that it seemed likely, she wasn't sure that was what she wanted. In fact, right then, she didn't know what she wanted.

Confused and troubled, she followed him into the living room, enjoying again the feeling of quiet soli-tude that struck her the first time. It felt like coming home—a feeling she hadn't had since she'd left the Corbetts' house and Gold Peak behind her.

The dogs frolicked around her until Cully ordered them to lie down. He seemed ill at ease and avoided meeting her gaze. She sat down at the end of a couch and Rags immediately threw himself down on the floor at her feet.

Cully picked up a pile of magazines, straightened them and put them down again. "Glass of wine?" he offered without looking at her.

"Thanks, I'd like that. Is there anything I can do?"

"No, thanks. I can manage." He gestured at the dogs who were now both lolling at her feet. "Don't let them jump up on the couches. Lyla wails like a cat in heat if she finds a dog hair on them. Just kick 'em out if they get to be a nuisance.''

He disappeared and she let out her breath. She prayed that he'd keep his distance. That he wouldn't be tempted to kiss her again. Because if he did, she wasn't sure how strong she could be.

He could still set her on fire with one meaningful look. He'd changed in so many ways but now that the tough shell was beginning to crack, it made him all the more appealing.

His strength, the integrity and deep concern for his fellow man that had always been an inherent part of him had attracted her long ago. She had forgotten what a powerful appeal that held for her. He was a good man both in his life and in his job. She only had to watch him with others to know that. People respected his judgement and heeded his advice.

He'd matured since she'd left, grown more confident. A man to be reckoned with. A forceful man, yet not in the way that Brandon had been.

Cully wouldn't control her life. He wouldn't dictate and bully, or threaten to get his way. He would share his life with her, not try to rule hers. He wouldn't be a master. He would be a lover. A partner. A soul mate.

Damn! She was falling into the trap again. She saw in Cully the qualities she'd thought she'd seen in Brandon and she had been badly mistaken. What she thought had been love on her part had been nothing more than her intense need for approval. As for Brandon, he was incapable of loving. Yet she'd truly believed that he'd loved her.

Now there was Cully, with his determination to

take care of her, protect her, be there for her. And she was responding to it the same way she had all those years ago. If she'd truly loved him back then, she wouldn't have left him to go to the city. If he'd truly loved her, he would have gone with her.

Thoroughly confused by her thoughts, she got up and wandered over to the fireplace. The landscape hanging above it was beautiful. A setting sun, half-hidden by the mountains, coloring the sky with broad bands of gold and purple. She could imagine how Cully would miss the land if he moved to the city. How miserable he must have been as a child, confined to the dusty, crowded streets, torn from the open skies, the distant mountains, the life he loved so much.

She could understand why he wouldn't want to go back to that life. But wasn't that what love was, sacrificing everything for each other? Neither of them had been willing to do that back then. And now? Was it really any different? Was all they had between them really nothing more than physical attraction, a need that could be fulfilled with a night of passion?

His voice startled her out of her thoughts. "Pretty, isn't it. It's the same view you can see from these windows in daylight."

He'd come up behind her and was standing a little too close. Still unsettled by her thoughts, she moved away from him. Panic surged through her, obliterating her thoughts, confusing her mind. She needed time. Time to sort out her feelings. Time to understand his. "I…I've changed my mind," she said quickly. "I'm really tired. If you don't mind, I'd like to go to my room."

If he was disappointed, he gave no sign. "Oh, sure." He placed the glasses on the glass coffee table. "I'll show you where it is."

She would have preferred to find it herself but that would seem childish. So she followed him meekly up the stairs, praying that he wouldn't make things awkward for them.

By the time he paused in front of the room at the end of the hallway, her heart thumped so hard she had difficulty breathing. She should never have come back to the ranch with him. She should have insisted on going to a hotel in Rapid City.

"This is Lyla's favorite room," Cully announced, as he threw open the door. "She calls it the blue room." He stepped inside and switched on a bedside lamp.

She'd seen the room yesterday when Cully had taken her on a tour of the house. She'd fallen in love with it right away. Her garment bag, now held together with swathes of duct tape, sat on the bed next to the empty canvas bag. The pale blue bedspread, dotted with yellow daises, matched the curtains at the window. The darker blue carpet was thick enough to bury bare toes.

The lamp, with its blue and white shade, stood over a fluffy blue rabbit wearing a yellow ribbon. Ginny picked it up, unable to resist a smile. "Is this a relic from your past?"

She looked up to find Cully's dark gaze intent on her face and her heart turned over.

"No," he said, his voice husky with some emotion she didn't want to explore. "Lyla bought it. She

helped with the decorating and thought a soft toy
would make the room look more liveable.''

"She was right." Ginny put the rabbit down and
wandered around the room, every nerve in her body
quivering with expectation. "This is very nice." Her
tongue seemed too big for her mouth. She sounded
stilted. She tried to put more warmth into her voice.
"Thank you, Cully. I appreciate everything you're
doing for me."

He looked at her, his expression grave and his gaze
burned into her soul. "You know where the bathroom
is?"

She nodded.

"Okay, then…" He turned to leave, then paused,
as if about to add something and her heart stopped
beating. Then, without looking at her, he muttered,
"Good night, Ginny. Sleep well." He left so quickly
she was still holding her breath when the door closed
behind him.

She should be glad he was being a gentleman, she
told herself. She should but she wasn't. After all that
hoping and praying that he wouldn't try to kiss her
again, now that he'd left her alone she felt let down.
Disappointed, if she was truly honest with herself.

She was acting like an adolescent and couldn't
seem to help it. Damn Cully. And herself for the in-
secure, doubting person that she had turned into. Was
this what Brandon had done to her? Made her doubt
her own judgement? What had happened to the Ginny
Matthews who was going to conquer the world?
Where had all that confidence and rebellion gone?
What was it Cully had said? *He's changed you, made*

you afraid. The Ginny I knew was never afraid of anything. Or anyone.

He was right. She was afraid. Of her own emotions. Of making another mistake.

In an effort to banish her turbulent thoughts, she took a relaxing shower, then climbed into bed. Now she was really tired. Exhausted. After all the emotional upheaval of this long, long day, all she wanted was to sleep, to forget for a little while her turmoil over her feelings for Cully. Forget that someone out there wanted her dead.

THREE HOURS LATER Cully still sat in front of the fireplace nursing a beer. He knew it would be a waste of time to go to bed. He wasn't going to sleep. There was just too much on his mind. Even the shower he'd taken earlier hadn't relaxed him.

He'd gone over and over the events of the day. Every time he'd tried to make some sense of what had happened—the tense moments on the mountain when they'd almost gone over the side, the shooting of Ben Wetherby and Sally's boyfriend stealing her car, leaving her with the van that had threatened them earlier—all of it became a jumble in his mind.

To make matters worse, the only clear thoughts he had were of Ginny and how much his body ached with the need to make love to her. The knowledge that she was on the floor above him, lying alone in that big bed, just about tied his guts in knots. He'd had to tear himself away from her earlier.

There'd been a couple of times that day when he'd been driven to the very edge of his limits, when he'd felt his willpower slipping and his mind losing the control he'd always relied on. Only Ginny could do that to him.

Puffing out his breath, he buried his face in his hands. He'd be an idiot to let himself get that close to losing it again.

Okay, so he had an idea she was as willing as he was to revisit the past but what about afterward? What about later? Did he really think that one night was going to change anything? It certainly hadn't before. Was he kidding himself by thinking that this time around, maybe it would be different? He just didn't know the answer to that but hell, he'd give his right arm for the chance to find out.

But then when he'd looked at her sitting on the edge of the bed, looking so vulnerable, so tense, he'd known this wasn't the time. Maybe there'd be a time for them after this was over. Maybe not. Maybe her life in the city had stretched a gulf between them that was too wide to cross.

"Damn." He lifted his head and reached for his beer. He'd brought her back to the ranch so he could protect her from whoever out there was trying to hurt her. What kind of a cop would he be if he let his personal feelings get in the way of his job? A useless cop, that's what. Personal feelings clouded judgement, slowed down reflexes, made him think too much instead of relying on instinct.

No, if there was ever going to be anything between them and at this point he couldn't see much chance of that, it would have to wait until this case was over. It was the only sane thing to do. He drained the last of his beer and got to his feet. If he wanted a clear mind in the morning, he'd better get some sleep.

The dogs stirred and Rags whined.

"Okay boys." He snapped his fingers at them. "One quick turn around the house, then we bed down for the night."

Rags leaped to his feet, tail wagging, and Puddles scrambled up beside him. Running for the door, with both dogs ahead of him, Cully put his finger to his lips. "Shsh! No barking. We don't want to wake up our guest." He opened the door and let them out, where they raced joyfully to the side of the house, dashed up to the thick trunk of a pine and promptly lifted a leg.

Cully strolled after them, still wrestling with his tangled thoughts. He had to find out what Brandon Pierce had been involved in if he had any hope of finding the connection to Ginny. It had to be something big. The most logical place to start seemed to be Pierce's house in Phoenix. He'd have to get a warrant to search it. Maybe take Ginny along, she'd know the layout and the most likely places to look for clues to Pierce's movements the past six months. Somehow, somewhere, lay the answers. He just had to look for them.

Realizing he'd walked around the house twice, he whistled to the dogs. They came slowly, reluctantly, wandering toward him with a resignation that clearly said they knew it was time to go back in.

He opened the door and let them run ahead of him. The dogs had baskets in the kitchen and he waited for them to settle down. He was about to leave when Rags lifted his head and uttered a low growl in his throat.

Pausing at the door, Cully looked back at him. "What is it, boy?"

Rags's ears pricked up and he uttered a soft whine.

Now Cully could hear what the dog had heard. A low moaning, followed by a shrill cry. The noises came from upstairs. *Ginny.*

Cully's body moved the instant his mind registered the significance of the sounds. He plunged through the door, slamming it behind him. Shut inside the kitchen, Rags barked and Puddles joined in but Cully was halfway up the stairs, taking them two at a time.

He reached the upper hallway and now he could hear her more clearly.

"No, no, please, not again. Don't hurt me. Please…"

He burst through the door, not knowing what to expect, his body braced for anything. He heard her scream, a shrill sound that tore through his gut like a buzz saw. The light from the hallway spilled across the bed, reflecting on her white face as she sat upright, her eyes wide with terror, staring at him as if he were about to attack her.

Relief exploded in his chest when he realized she was alone and safe. She'd been dreaming. "It's okay, Ginny," he said unsteadily. "It's only me. You had a bad dream, that's all."

For a moment he thought she hadn't understood him but then she whimpered and he saw tears shining on her cheeks. Something else burst inside him. Something that up until now had held up the barriers of self-control and willpower. It was as if all his doubts, all his self-warnings were being washed away by a great tide of emotion. Helpless to stop himself, he sat on the bed and cradled her in his arms.

She clung to him, her body trembling so much he thought she must be cold. He stroked her hair, murmuring senseless words and broken sentences, until the trembling slowed then stopped altogether.

She drew back and looked up at him. "Nightmare," she said simply.

"I know. I'm sorry." He pressed his lips to her damp forehead. "Feel better now?"

She nodded but her arms still clung to his shoulders as if she were afraid to let go.

He became conscious of her body, warm and soft beneath the T-shirt she wore. He was acutely aware that she wore nothing beneath it. Warning signals were going off all over his body but he was past listening to them. He was past anything except this deep, intense longing to kiss her, to run his hands over her body, to feel again the incredible pleasure of fitting himself inside her.

Hardly daring to breathe in case he should break the spell, he traced his lips down to her cheek, the corner of her mouth. He felt her tense and for one devastating second thought she would draw back but then she moved her head and locked her mouth on his.

The heat surged up through his veins, blasting all coherent thought from his mind. He'd wanted her so badly all day long and now she was his. He could feel it in her kiss, in her eager fingers tugging at his shirt, in her swelling breasts beneath his hands.

He slid off the bed and shed his clothes, flinging

them aside in his haste to get back to her before she changed her mind.

She sat watching him, her gaze lingering on his body all the way down to his knees. That was more erotic than anything he'd ever known before. He couldn't wait to get back to her.

The bed creaked as he sat down beside her. Now it was his turn to watch as she pulled off her T-shirt and bared her breasts.

His breath seemed caught in his throat and his lungs ached with the need for air. In all of his life he had never seen anything so breathtaking. He wouldn't have thought it possible but she was even more beautiful than he remembered.

He leaned forward and touched her lips with his and passion once more exploded in his gut. With a groan that contained all the pent-up hunger he'd held back for so long, he pulled her against him. Her body was silky smooth and first his hands, then his mouth, sought the firm curves of her breasts, her hips, her thighs.

The soft sounds she made drove him wild. He fought his own need, anxious to answer the demands of her body, now arching under his touch. Memory vanished under the amazing sensations of the present moment. There had never been a past, a separation, a breaking of the ties. They were and always had been and always would be, a single unity, bound by the strange, primitive laws that governed the mating of a man and his woman.

She was ready, her cries louder, her thrashing body straining for release. He touched her and her body arched, tensed and then, with a heart-shattering cry, she relaxed, panting for breath, the tears still wet on her face.

He didn't give her time to rest. His own body throbbed with the agony of need and he could wait no longer. She accepted him eagerly, folding her legs around his hips as he entered her. Stars danced in his head and he fought to hold back until he was helpless to halt the fierce torrent of emotion that threatened to consume him.

She rocked with him, their bodies joined in a frantic rhythm that shook the bed. Her hand clutched the pillow next to her face and he locked his fingers over hers, the blood pounding in his head as his hips strained for the final release. Then, at long last, they were there…together…rocketing through space and floating free.

He lay for a long time after she fell asleep, soaking in the pleasure of holding her naked body in his arms. He wanted to hold on to every moment, afraid that if he didn't, the time would slip away and once more he'd be left with only memories.

He was afraid to hope, afraid to speculate, to dream. He'd had dreams once before and they had been cruelly shattered. He'd laid his heart on the line, only to have it crushed. All he could do was enjoy the moment right now and try not to think about what tomorrow might bring.

GINNY OPENED her eyes, certain at first that she'd dreamed Cully had made love to her the night before. Seconds later she felt the warmth of his body next to hers and carefully turned her head.

He lay on his back, his eyes closed, his breathing

deep and even. She wanted to smooth her hand over his bare shoulder, run her fingers across his shadowed jaw but was reluctant to spoil the sleep that had softened the hard, tense lines of his face.

He looked younger, sensitive, totally endearing. The rush of tenderness took her by surprise. For some strange reason, she felt tears on her lashes.

If only she could be sure that what they had was enough. He hadn't mentioned love at all. But if it came to that, could she love him enough to bury herself once more in a small town like Gold Peak?

The thought depressed her but when she thought about leaving and never seeing him again, the thought of that was far more devastating.

Had she been kidding herself that she was happy in Philadelphia? Did she really enjoy city life all that much, with its choking fumes, the constant rush, the transit jammed with warm bodies at the end of an exhausting day, the roar of traffic, blaring horns and grating rock music from too loud radios? Did she really like the loneliness, or had she simply been thankful for the freedom of being her own person once more, safe from the cruel abuse of her bullying husband?

She glanced again at Cully, so peaceful in his sleep. She needed to think, to sort out her feelings and she couldn't do it lying next to his warm, naked body. It was too distracting. Too easy to remember him as he was last night, wild in his excitement, so giving, so passionate. She needed to put some space between them. She needed to think things out.

Carefully she slipped out of bed, grabbed up some clean clothes and crept from the room. In the bathroom she showered, dressed hurriedly, then stole down the stairs to the front door.

She heard Rags whine as she opened the door and winced, hoping he wouldn't bark and wake up Cully. The thought prompted her to hunt in her purse for something to write on. Finding her release paper from the hospital, she scribbled across the top of the page. *Gone for a drive. See you later.*

She had always been able to think more clearly when she was driving. Maybe it would work for her this time and help her make a decision she knew might very well change her life forever. That wasn't a decision to be made lightly. Yet she didn't have a whole lot of time to make it. She had a job waiting for her in Philadelphia and if she didn't get back to it soon, they would have to replace her.

She needed to decide now what she wanted to do. Go back to the new life she'd created for herself, or stay in Gold Peak in the hope that she might have a future with Cully.

She'd spotted her rental car parked in front of the house last night. It started right away, much to her relief. She thought she heard Rags bark as she pulled away and hoped again that he wouldn't wake up Cully. It must have been close to dawn before he'd gotten any sleep.

She wound down the windows and took the highway fast, trying to clear her head so that she could think more clearly. She tried to imagine herself living in Gold Peak and made herself remember everything about living in Philadelphia. Not just the advantages but the drawbacks, as well.

Deep in thought, she slowed down for a crossroad

and realized she was only a mile or two from the graveyard. Impulse made her turn the wheel and follow the road up the hill.

She'd always been able to talk to Mabel, about anything. Maybe it would help to visit the grave again and talk out loud. Perhaps then she'd find the answers she needed.

A few minutes later she parked the car at the gates of the graveyard and went in search of the two graves. It was nice they had been buried side by side, she reflected as she reached the twin headstone. It must be comforting to know they would be together for all eternity.

She knelt in the damp grass and straightened the flowers someone had placed in vases on the grave. They looked faded and she made a mental note to buy some more when she went back to town.

"Hi Mabel," she said, feeling a little self-conscious. "I'm back. I'm having a problem with a decision, and I need to talk to you about it." As she talked, her confidence grew and before long, the answer came to her, so clearly she couldn't imagine why she hadn't thought of it earlier.

"I knew you'd help me," she said, as she got to her feet. "Thank you both."

When a voice answered her, she froze.

"It's really too bad they're not here to help you now."

She hadn't heard footsteps on the grass behind her. She hadn't been aware of his presence until he'd spoken. It wasn't the fact that he'd snuck up on her that horrified her, though that was shocking enough. It was his voice that struck stark, cold terror in her heart.

Slowly she turned to face him, her mind totally
unable to accept what she'd heard. In an ice-cold daze
she stared at the familiar face, all coherent thought
blasted from her mind.

"Good morning, Virginia," he said pleasantly.
"It's so good to see you."

As the ground tilted away from her, she grappled
with the impossible. The man who stood in front of
her, his mouth stretched in a ghastly grin, was the one
man on earth she had expected never to set eyes on
again.

Chapter Fourteen

Cully dragged himself out of a pleasant dream, where he was wandering down a deserted beach, hand in hand with Ginny, while the dogs dashed ahead, barking and leaping into the waves.

Squinting through half-closed lids, he realized three things at once. He was in the wrong room, the daylight was much brighter than it should be and the dogs were barking downstairs.

In the next instant he remembered something else. He twisted his head, his excitement vanishing at the sight of the empty space next to him. Last night he'd looked forward to waking up with her this morning and making love with her all over again. To find her gone was a shattering disappointment.

He wondered where she was. In the bathroom maybe? Though by the sound of the frantic barking going on downstairs, she was probably down there playing with them. Maybe she'd gone down to make coffee. He sniffed the air but could detect no pleasant aroma drifting up the stairs.

Anxious to see her again he leaped from the bed, pulled on his pants and headed out the door. Halfway down the stairs, he frowned. The dogs barking sounded muffled, as if they were still shut up in the kitchen.

He tried to ignore the niggling uneasiness in the pit of his stomach as he ran down the rest of the stairs and threw open the kitchen door.

Rags almost knocked him over in his haste to get out. Puddles bounced along behind him, uttering little yaps of annoyance. A quick look around the kitchen confirmed what he'd already suspected. Ginny wasn't in there.

For the first time he got a good look at the clock and winced. He'd overslept. It was almost eight-thirty. Where in heck was Ginny?

Rags sat at the front door, whining. Cully opened it and let both dogs out then went into the living room. He spotted the note right away, lying on the coffee table. His stomach took a nosedive. She'd gone. The least she could have done was said good-bye in person.

He couldn't bring himself to read the note. He could imagine what it said. *This isn't going to work. I'm going back where I belong, to my life in the city.* Or words that meant the same thing. By now she was probably at the airport, on her way back to the east coast.

He tried to tell himself she was safer there, where no one knew how to find her. It didn't help the aching emptiness in his stomach. He filled the coffee machine and plugged it in. Then he went upstairs and took a long shower. By the time he stepped out of it, he was more or less resigned. It hurt, yes. It hurt like hell. But he'd more or less expected it.

He'd known, ever since she'd come home, that she wasn't going to stay. How could she? The town had been too small for her when she was just a kid. Now that she was used to living in the big, bad city, it would be that much harder for her to break away and come back to Gold Peak. She was right. Her job was there. Her life was there. And he had no right to try to take that away from her.

He dressed quickly, then realized he'd left his shoes and his watch in her bedroom. No, the blue room. He had to stop thinking about it as her room.

Stepping into that room was a painful move. He saw his crumpled clothes on the floor and flinched as if someone had hit him in the stomach. Then he saw something else. The T-shirt Ginny had taken off in front of him last night.

Frowning, he lunged across the bed, looked over the side and saw what he'd missed earlier. Her canvas bag and the torn garment bag were lying on the floor. She hadn't left him after all.

His relief and hope were so intense that for a moment he forgot what else that might mean. When the cold reality dawned on him he jumped up from the bed and bounded down the stairs. He could hear the dogs scratching to come in but he was intent on one thing.

He snatched up the note and read it. Cursing loud and lustily, he went to let the dogs in then headed for the phone. He called the Red Steer, his office, the three beauty shops in town, Neil Baumann and his two deputies, leaving orders that if they should see Ginny, to keep her there until he got there. Jed was still at the hospital. Ben Wetherby was holding his own, he told Cully, but was still in a coma.

It was his fault, Cully told himself as he drove like a maniac into town. He should have ordered Ginny to stay with him. He'd played down the danger of her being out alone for fear of frightening her too much. Now she was out there somewhere, with a dangerous killer looking for her.

Anxiously he scanned the highway as he headed into town, hoping against hope to see her car. When he got to his office and found no messages waiting for him, he started worrying in earnest. She'd gone for a drive, she said. *Where?*

He glanced up at the clock then called the ranch.

Lyla answered, sounding breathless. "I just got here," she said, when he asked her if Ginny was there. "Let me look."

He waited in a fever of impatience until he heard the housekeeper's voice again. "No, Sheriff, she's not here. I've looked all over the house. Her things are still here, though. Will she be staying tonight?"

"I hope so." He swallowed down the fear. "Look, Lyla, if she comes back there, tell her to call me right away."

"Of course." Lyla sounded worried. "There's nothing wrong, is there?"

He forced a light note in his voice. "No, don't worry. She's just gone for a drive. I'm sure she'll be back there soon."

"I sure hope so. What with all these dreadful things going on in town lately, I don't know if anyone is safe out there."

He hung up, forcing himself to calm down. He'd

specifically warned her about going to the Corbett house alone. He couldn't imagine her going up there without him, especially after what had happened to Ben Wetherby. He looked at the clock. Maybe he should send Cory up there to look.

He was about to call him when the phone rang, making him jump. Praying it was Ginny, he said sharply, "Sheriff Black."

An unfamiliar voice greeted him. "This is Collins, NDI."

His brain was scrambled. He couldn't think straight. He had no idea what the initials stood for. "Huh?"

"Nevada Division of Investigations," the voice explained with exaggerated patience. "You were enquiring yesterday about David Petersen?"

Cully's mind cleared at once. "Yeah, I was. I understand he's a missing person."

"Well, not anymore. His body was discovered early this morning in a ditch. Rural road, been there for a few days. Looks like the victim of a hit-and-run."

Cully's fingers tapped hard on his desk. "What did this guy look like?"

"A mess," Collins said dryly.

"No, I mean, his physical appearance."

"Oh, I thought you knew him."

"Only by name."

"Well, he's late-thirties, dark-blond hair, though he's lost most of it, blue eyes, big gut, weighs around two hundred pounds. That your guy?"

Cully let out his breath. "No, I guess not. But thanks for the information."

"Sure. If you need anything else, you can get in touch with me at this number."

Cully wrote the number down and hung up. Another possible death to hang on this guy. There was no point in telling Nevada that until he was sure. One thing he could be sure of was that this guy meant business.

He shoved his chair back, grabbed his hat and headed for the door. Every minute that Ginny was out there put her in more danger. How long ago had she left the house that morning? Two hours? Three? Four? Whatever it was, it was long enough for her to be in real trouble.

GINNY SAT with her shoulder blades pressed against the wall of the basement, her mind still frozen in shock. Not for one moment had she considered the possibility that Brandon was still alive.

She still found it impossible to believe that the man she'd married and believed she'd loved, the man with whom she'd danced, slept and traveled half the world had murdered her beloved foster parents in cold blood.

She closed her mind against the ugly accusations he'd flung at her as he'd gagged her, then bound her hands and feet before throwing her in the dark blue car that he'd stolen from Sally.

She hadn't been all that surprised when he'd brought her back to the Corbetts' house. She'd half hoped that at least one of Cully's deputies would be still conducting an investigation but Brandon was too smart to walk into a trap like that. He must have known the investigation was wrapped up last night.

From what he'd told her, he'd gone to a lot of trouble to find her. He'd staged his own death, killing the unsuspecting passenger he'd picked up at the last minute, a young man applying for a job as his assistant. He'd hiked out of the area and hitched a ride with David Petersen.

He hadn't meant to kill the salesman, he'd told Ginny, as if that exonerated him from the rest of the deaths. Apparently Petersen had stood in front of him, trying to stop him from stealing the van and all his ID. Brandon had expected him to jump out of the way at the last minute but either he was too stubborn or hadn't been quite fast enough. Brandon had driven right over him.

He'd gone back to see if he was dead, then had shoved him in a ditch. He'd called the Corbetts, expecting them to give him his wife's address. When they couldn't, he'd driven to Gold Peak, intending to beat it out of them.

Ginny closed her eyes. Four people dead and another lying in a hospital bed. And, if he managed to carry out the threat he'd snarled at her just before leaving, there'd be two more deaths on his hands.

Brandon had been following her movements, both physically and through Sally, ever since she'd arrived in Gold Peak. He knew that she'd spent last night at the ranch. He was mad with jealousy. Apparently he had been ever since he'd seen her with Cully in the Red Steer that first night.

She'd made the mistake of telling Brandon all about Cully and her life in Gold Peak. That's why he'd befriended Sally. Knowing they had been best friends, he'd relied on Sally to keep him informed.

But in the end he hadn't needed her. Gold Peak was a small town. All he'd had to do was keep his ears open. Thank God he hadn't hurt Sally. She'd had a lucky escape.

Ginny stared down at her bound feet, fighting the fear that was threatening to overwhelm her. Her hands, bound behind her, were beginning to lose all sensation. He'd outlined, in lurid detail, everything he planned to do to her before he killed her. If she hadn't had a scarf stuffed in her mouth, she would have thrown up all over him.

He'd left, saying he wanted to give her time to think about what he had in store for her. The suffocating gag was so tight she wondered if she'd choke to death before he returned. Where had he gone, anyway? The devastating fear that he'd gone to kill Cully and was coming back to gloat about it almost destroyed her. If only she could get free, get out of there, get help and warn him.

She couldn't believe this was happening. After all this time she'd finally found the answers she'd been looking for and the thought that it could be too late, that she'd never get the chance to share them with Cully tore her apart.

She leaned back against the wall and winced as something poked painfully into her back. It had to be a nail. She shifted to her right and turned her head as far as the scarf would allow. The tiny window above her head was at ground level outside. It was so caked with mud and dirt that little light filtered through. Even so, it was enough to reveal the large nail sticking out of the wall just below her shoulder blades.

She leaned against it with her elbow. It was firmly

embedded in the wall. The head was about half an inch across.

Hope stirred, though she was wary of getting too excited. Even if she could reach it with her bound wrists, it would take forever to saw through the duct tape binding her.

Leaning forward, she lifted her hands up behind her as far as they would go. It took several tries before she located the nail but finally it caught in the tape and she began moving her hands back and forth, fast and furious at first, then more slowly as her muscles cramped in protest.

Many times she had to stop and wait for the pain to subside before she could resume the frantic sawing that was her only hope of getting free. Finally, just when she was on the point of giving up, she felt the tape rip. Her strength renewed by the hope surging in her, she sawed and sawed until, with a cry of triumph, she dragged her wrists apart.

Agonizing pain shot up her arms and through her fingers, forcing her to cry out. She massaged her aching muscles and after a while regained enough feeling in her hands to remove the scarf and rip the tape from her ankles.

Being able to breathe properly more than made up for the pain she endured while the blood rushed back into her feet. Her legs felt like sticks of wilted celery when she pulled herself upright and she had to stamp her feet hard to get circulation in them again. By the time the tingling finally stopped, she was seething with impatience.

She was halfway up the basement steps when it occurred to her that Brandon could still be in the house. She froze, then reasoned that if he were there he surely would have heard her stamping around down there and would come down to investigate.

Feeling cold at her carelessness, she warned herself to be more cautious. Quietly she turned the handle of the door at the top of the steps. Fear followed quickly on frustration when she realized it was locked.

She dashed down the steps again, heedless of the dark and darted back to the window. Even if she could have opened it, it was far too small to squeeze through. Even as the reality hit her, she heard a door slam overhead. He was back. And she was trapped.

CULLY HAD DRIVEN the length of town, stopping only to call in at various places to ask if anyone had seen Ginny's car. He already had an APB out on Sally's Mazda but so far no one had called in. Jed and Cory were cruising the side streets, though Cully couldn't imagine why she would drive down any of them.

What worried him was the possibility that she'd gone into Rapid City, in which case she'd be tough to find. He'd just about run out of places to look for her. Only two were left in town that he could think of. One of them was the Corbett house. He was reluctant to waste time going up there, pretty sure that it would be the last place she'd go.

So instead, he headed out to the graveyard. As he crested the hill he had a clear view of the parking spaces outside the gate. There was only one car parked there. A blue Mazda.

He screeched to a halt beside it. It was Sally's car, all right. He recognized it instantly. He frowned, scanning the cemetery for any signs of life. Nothing moved, except the branches of the cottonwoods in the cool wind.

His heart thudded with anxiety. Had the killer abandoned the car and stolen something else? But why here? It was just too much of a coincidence. There could be only one explanation. Ginny had come back here, probably to say goodbye before she left town for good. The killer must have grabbed her and taken her in her car.

His heart thudded to his boots. *Where would he take her? Had he already killed her?* No, he wouldn't let himself consider that. She had to be alive. She had to be. There was one possibility but he'd be taking a chance going all the way up there. If she wasn't there, he'd have wasted precious time.

Struggling with indecision, he knew it was his only option. The killer had been to the house before. He had to rule it out before he could concentrate on anything else.

He flung himself back in the Jeep, radioed a message to Cory and headed for the Corbetts' house.

THE FOOTSTEPS echoed above Ginny's head, drawing closer to the door. She gripped the heavy shovel that moments ago had been leaning against the wall. If she had the strength to swing it, it would make a formidable weapon.

Her advantage would be surprise. He thought she was still tied up. She moved farther back into the shadows behind the steps. She'd get one chance and one chance only. If she missed, she'd be helpless against his strength.

Balancing the unwieldy shovel in her hands, she

waited, heart thumping, her nerves screaming with tension.

The door opened. He'd left the lights on in the hallway and through the gaps in the steps she watched his shoes stepping down. He was halfway down when he called out to her, making her jump so violently she almost dropped the shovel.

"Hello, Virginia. I've come back as I promised. The time has come to play our little game."

Her hands started shaking uncontrollably and she took a firmer grip on the handle. He stepped down, slowly and surely, even though his sight had to be hampered by the darkness. He hadn't had time to adjust yet, not like her. She could see better than he could.

The knowledge gave her courage. She waited, poised to strike, as he paused, one hand outstretched in front of him to pull the string on the light. When his fingers didn't connect, he muttered a surprised curse.

If she hadn't been so scared she would have smiled. Just moments earlier she'd tugged the light on, then tugged it off again, putting all her weight on the string until it had snapped and collapsed in her hand.

She watched him step forward, off the last step, his hand still groping for the string. One step forward, then two.

"What the—?" He started to turn around and she sprang into action.

One wild swing at his head, perfectly timed. He practically walked into it. He went down like a felled tree.

He was blocking the steps. She'd have to step over him.

She waited, watching, shovel poised. He didn't move. Had she killed him? Her stomach heaved until she reminded herself of everything he'd done. He deserved to die.

One more second. Two. Still he didn't move.

She laid down the shovel. Raised a foot and stepped over him. Sensing freedom, she surged forward.

Without warning, something clamped around her ankle.

His hand, cold and as relentless as steel.

She screamed. Tugged and tugged to be free. She lashed out with her foot but he was already on his knees, grabbing her, holding her, his hand on her throat. She tried to scream again but all that came out was a horrible gurgle.

Dimly she heard a crash above her head. The door at the top of the steps swung open. Smashed against the wall. She heard Cully's voice, low and harsh with suppressed fury.

"Let her go. *Now!* It's all over."

The pressure on her throat grew tighter and she couldn't swallow. Couldn't breathe. Brandon's cruel hands dragged her up against him, turning her around to face the steps, one arm still clamped around her throat. "Go ahead," he snarled. "Shoot. You'll have to go through my wife to get me."

In the light from the hallway Ginny saw shock transform Cully's face as the truth sank in. He hesitated and she felt Brandon's free hand move at her side. Light gleamed on the ugly squat gun in his hand.

She tried to scream a warning but all she could manage was a choking gasp. She lunged sideways, throwing all her weight on Brandon's arm just as he fired. The bullet ricocheted off the wall.

She heard Cully yell and for a horrible moment thought he'd been hit. Instead of falling, however, he leaped forward. His body seemed to sail through the air and again Brandon fired, despite her struggles to prevent him.

The full weight of Cully's body landed on her, forcing the breath out of her lungs. Brandon dropped the gun, staggered back and went down, taking her with him. Dazed and choking, she realized the pressure on her throat was gone. She wriggled free of the two men, while they struggled for the gun still in Cully's hand.

She scrambled to her feet, gasping for breath. Still locked in savage combat, the two men struggled to their feet then disappeared around the corner. Almost immediately, a deafening report burst in her ears, making her head sing.

She waited in the deathly silence that followed, trembling and afraid. No one moved. Fearfully she took a step forward. "Cully?"

A tall figure stepped around the corner. A stray ray of sunshine had fought its way through the dust-grimed window. It gleamed on the gun in his hand.

"Sorry, my dear," Brandon said nastily. "Your boyfriend can't answer you. Now you can both rot in hell together. Too bad we won't get to play our little game as I promised, but I'm running out of time." He aimed the gun at her and even in the half-light she could see the cold, round barrel pointing straight at her head.

She shut her eyes. What did it matter now, anyway. Brandon had killed Cully. Everyone who mattered to her had been wiped out now. Everyone. There was nothing left.

Bracing herself, she heard the deafening blast ringing in her ears again. It was a moment or two before she realized she wasn't hit. He must have missed. She was braced for him to shoot again. When it didn't come she opened her eyes.

Looking down, she saw him on the floor and in the dim light she could see a spreading puddle of dark liquid. Someone else moved then and stepped into the dim light, a gun held steadily in his hand.

Cully! With a cry she ran toward him, then pulled back with a gasp of horror when she saw the dark stain on his forehead.

"It's okay. It's only a scratch." He held out his arm. "Are you all right?"

No, she wasn't all right. She'd been through hell and back.

She'd lost two people she'd loved with all her heart. She'd thought she'd lost the one person in the world she had left to love. She tried to speak, cleared her throat and tried again. "What kept you?" she said and went into his arms.

IT WAS LATE that evening before Ginny's voice sounded normal again. She'd enjoyed a wonderful meal of trout almondine and a mouthwatering tiramisu made from scratch. Two glasses of wine had finally calmed her nerves and she sat on the couch in

Cully's living room, her shoulder resting on his chest, while the dogs lay snoring at their feet.

She'd been listening to Cully's account of that morning and his harrowing search for her.

"You can't begin to imagine how I felt," he said, "seeing that monster's hands around your throat and then finding out it was your husband. My finger itched to pull the trigger, but I was afraid of hitting you."

"I know." Ginny shuddered. "I just can't believe that he's dead and it's all over. I don't have to be frightened of him anymore."

"Yeah, lucky I'd kicked his gun into the corner while we were struggling on the floor. It took me a while to find it. It was a close call. Too close." His arm tightened around her. "Another few seconds and I'd have been too late."

"I thought he'd killed you." She felt sick, remembering that awful moment. "How's your head feel?"

"Apart from a slight headache, not bad. The doc said it should heal up in a few days. I was lucky, the bullet just grazed my forehead. An inch to the left and I wouldn't have woken up."

She buried her face in his shirt. "I don't want to think about it."

"Then don't. Let's change the subject."

"Okay. I'm glad that Old Man Wetherby is going to be all right."

"Me, too. It'll be a while before he's up and around, but he'll make it."

"We should visit him."

"Sounds like a good idea." He shifted his position, then said carefully, "You gonna be around long enough to do that?"

Her heart stalled for a second or two. It was now or never.

"I've been thinking a lot about it lately. When I sell the Corbetts' house I'll have the capital to start a business of my own. I was thinking maybe a clothing store."

"Oh." He was quiet for a moment, then to her utter astonishment he said, "I've been thinking, too. I thought I might try for a job with the force in Philly. It would do me good to have a change of pace. I'm running out of challenges. Nothing ever happens in a small town. It's just been too quiet around here lately."

She sat up and stared at him. He looked a bit like a swashbuckling pirate with the bandage wound around his head. Her heart turned over with love. All her doubts had vanished with that one, incredible sacrifice he was willing to make for her.

"Oh, then we won't be seeing too much of each other," she said lightly. "I was planning to open a shop in Rapid City."

He seemed to be lost for words. She could read the hope in his eyes and her heart lifted with joy. "That's not too much of a commute," he said at last. "Maybe we could get together for dinner now and then."

Her heart seemed to be skipping all over the place. Steadily she met his gaze. "It would be even less of a commute if I lived here."

He gazed at her, conflicting expressions chasing across his face. Disbelief, hope, longing, she could see them all. Then a slow smile spread over his face, a smile so full of love she felt like crying. "Why, ma'am,'' he said softly, "are you suggesting what I think you're suggesting?''

She pretended to be concerned. "Would that hurt your reputation? I mean, I don't want to be responsible for wrecking your career.''

"I reckon we could find a way around that.'' He gently pushed her away from him and got to his feet. His face looked pale in the lamplight but there was no mistaking the intent in his eyes. "I don't have a ring right now, but we'll see to that tomorrow. In the meantime,'' he said as he slowly got down on one knee, "I've loved you ever since you were a skinny kid following me around like a puppy dog. There's never been anyone else. You're the only one in my heart, Ginny Matthews. I'd be real honored if you'd agree to be my wife.''

She smiled at him, her own heart so full she found it hard to find the words. "I've waited a lifetime for you to ask. Of course I will.''

"Good.'' He grinned at her. "Now help me up and I'll give you a sampling of what I have planned for you over the next hundred years.''

She stood, dragging him to his feet. "I seem to remember the doctor warning you about taking it easy for the next few days. No excitement.''

He folded his arms around her. "Yeah? Well, what do doctors know, anyway.'' His kiss, warm, demanding and full of promise sealed her happiness. Life would be good with Cully. Life would be very good. And she'd never run scared again.

SILHOUETTE®
INTRIGUE™

ROCKY MOUNTAIN MANHUNT
by Cassie Miles
Colorado Crime Consultants

When Kate Carradine woke up with no memories of who or where she was, only one thing was clear: someone was trying to kill her—and she had to go into hiding. Then suddenly, a sexy stranger materialised, offering his protection. But would Liam MacKenzie accept her once she regained her memory, or would he long for the wild woman he'd rescued?

DENIM DETECTIVE by Adrianne Lee
Cowboy Cops

Sheriff Beau Shanahan's life fell apart when his mistrust led to his family's demise. And then his wife returned—with a killer on her trail and the belief that their baby was alive. Would his mistakes cost him the two people he loved the most…again?

OUT FOR JUSTICE by Susan Kearney
Shotgun Sallys

Kelly McGovern suspected the town was covering up her brother's murder, and the one man the townsfolk didn't trust was the only one she wanted watching her back. Between dodging bullets and town interrogations, could she convince dangerous rebel Wade Lansing their attraction needed some private investigation of its own?

THE SEDGWICK CURSE by Shawna Delacorte
Eclipse

Donovan Sedgwick's great-grandfather had loved a woman with an obsession that had left them both dead and their families cursed. Now, a century later, Taylor MacKenzie invaded Donovan's life, questioning the Sedgwick curse and looking too beautiful to resist. When a rash of murders began, it seemed the past was repeating itself. But, this time, were Taylor and Donovan destined to love…or destined to die?

On sale from 16th June 2006

www.silhouette.co.uk

'It's scary just how good Tess Gerritsen is.'
—Harlan Coben

Twenty years after her father's plane crashed in the jungles of Southeast Asia, Willy Jane Maitland was finally tracking his last moves. She recognised the dangers, but her search for the truth about that fateful flight was the only thing that mattered.

Closing in on the events of that night, Willy realises that she is investigating secrets that people would kill to protect. And without knowing who to trust, the truth can be far from clear cut...

19th May 2006

A terror-inducing page-turner, *A PERFECT EVIL* offers a white-knuckle ride...

Serial killer Ronald Jeffreys was executed for three murders.

Three months after his death, the body of a boy is found, killed in the same style as Jeffreys' victims.

Is there a copycat killer on the loose?
Or is this the real thing?

Sheriff Nick Morrelli calls in one of the FBI's best criminal profilers, Maggie O'Dell. Together they start to uncover the gruesome picture of a killer and the terrible truth begins to come clear. Was Jeffreys convicted of crimes he didn't commit? Or has a cold-blooded killer been given the chance to perfect his crime?

MIRA

FREE!

2 Books
and a surprise gift!

We would like to take this opportunity to thank you for reading this Silhouette® book by offering you the chance to take TWO more specially selected titles from the Intrigue™ series absolutely FREE! We're also making this offer to introduce you to the benefits of the Reader Service™—

- ★ **FREE home delivery**
- ★ **FREE gifts and competitions**
- ★ **FREE monthly Newsletter**
- ★ **Exclusive Reader Service offers**
- ★ **Books available before they're in the shops**

Accepting these FREE books and gift places you under no obligation to buy. you may cancel at any time. even after receiving your free shipment. Simply complete your details below and return the entire page to the address below. You don't even need a stamp!

YES! Please send me 2 free Intrigue books and a surprise gift. I understand that unless you hear from me. I will receive 4 superb new titles every month for just £3.10 each. postage and packing free. I am under no obligation to purchase any books and may cancel my subscription at any time. The free books and gift will be mine to keep in any case.

16ZEF

Ms/Mrs/Miss/Mr ....Initials ....
BLOCK CAPITALS PLEASE
Surname ....
Address...

....
....Postcode ....

Send this whole page to:
UK: FREEPOST CN81, Croydon, CR9 3WZ